STAY ALIVE

Written by

Cathy Xinman

Contact

Email:xinmancathy@gmail.com

Email:cnawpress@gmail.com

Wechat:Xinman1225

STAY ALIVE

Written by

Cathy Xinman

Sycamore Books & Entertainment Publishing Inc.

Stay Alive
Cathy Xinman, author.
A Screenplay

Published by: Sycamore Books & Entertainment Publishing Inc.
Prepared for Publication: Canadian North America Writers Press Inc.
Interior Designer: Shi M. Wong
Author Photograph by: Yangyang

ISBN: 978-1-963840-04-9(Paperback)
ISBN (Ten Digits}:1-963840-04-9
ISBN: 978-1-963840-05-6(E-book)

Summary

"Stay Alive" is a deeply emotional and layered story that follows **April**, a young woman grappling with poverty, family turmoil, and her dreams of becoming a poet and playwright. The screenplay is a poignant exploration of **human resilience, the search for identity, and the power of art** in the face of life's hardships.

April's life is upended when her father, **Kong Fulai**, succumbs to gambling addiction, leading to financial ruin and domestic violence. After a violent confrontation at home, April leaves her family and embarks on a journey to find stability and meaning. She takes on various jobs, including working at a nursing home, a cemetery, and a restaurant owned by her aunt, **Xu Meili**. However, she faces constant setbacks, including unemployment, depression, and the emotional toll of her family's struggles.

Throughout her journey, April encounters a diverse cast of characters, each grappling with their own struggles. **Mike**, a mysterious man, becomes a significant figure in her life, offering both companionship and complications. **Homeless 404,** a former computer scientist now living on the streets, provides a poignant reflection on loss and redemption. April also interacts with **AI Onion** and **AI Jasmine**, two AI entities that appear through her experimental AI glasses. These AIs blur the lines between reality and virtuality, offering her guidance and companionship but also raising questions about the role of technology in human lives.

The screenplay delves into **family dysfunction**, as April's relationship with her parents is strained by her father's gambling and her mother's helplessness. Her aunt Xu Meili's decision to undergo euthanasia adds another layer of emotional complexity, forcing April to confront themes of loss, responsibility, and the fragility of life.

Despite the hardships, April's passion for poetry and playwriting remains a constant source of hope and self-expression. The story culminates in a powerful moment of redemption, as April and her friends perform a stage play, symbolizing her resilience and the transformative power of art.

Main Themes:

1. **Resilience and Survival**: April's journey is a testament to the human spirit's ability to endure and overcome adversity. Despite the

challenges she faces, she continues to fight for a better life.

2. **Family and Relationships**: The screenplay explores the complexities of family dynamics, including love, betrayal, and the struggle for reconciliation.

3. **Art and Self-Expression**: April's passion for poetry and playwriting serves as a central theme, highlighting the power of art to heal, inspire, and provide meaning in difficult times.

4. **Technology and Humanity**: The presence of AI Onion and AI Jasmine raises questions about the intersection of technology and human emotion, exploring how technology can both aid and complicate our lives.

5. **Loss and Redemption**: The story deals with themes of loss—both personal and familial—and the possibility of redemption through connection and creativity.

In conclusion, **"Stay Alive"** is a deeply moving story about a young woman's struggle to find her place in the world, navigate complex relationships, and hold onto her dreams in the face of overwhelming odds. The heart of the story lies in April's resilience, her pursuit of art, and her journey toward self-discovery.

[fade in]

1. Music. Title sequence:

The accompaniment starts with a sad tone and ends with strange and curious music. A girl, in her twenties, walks in the dark. Cat's eyes appear in front of her left and walks towards her hastily. She stops and shouts to the cat to stop. She is APRIL. The title is highly dynamic and appears in the ancient stone inscription essay. Calligraphies are carved on a drum-shaped granite stone. The MAIN TITLE appears on the screen with a strange sound, a sound carved on the stone.

Title sequence ends. The sound of rain and strong winds on the black screen…

The music fades.

2. I/E. APRIL'S HOME - NIGHT

Smashed dishes and broken porcelain, scattered food and glass fragments are everywhere. The noises of framed glass shattering on the carpet are heard. Then, a "bang" of the closing door follows. Someone walks out. JIA SHUYA sits on the messy floor, clenches her fists with both hands and hits herself on the head. Her eyes are stunned and dazed. She cries. APRIL enters from the outside and finds the blood on her mother's nose.

> **APRIL**
>
> Mom? What's wrong? Did he drink and hit you again?

> **JIA SHUYA**
>
> Why? Why is he like this? Why...? He just… left.

JIA SHUYA wails uncontrollably. The cellphone next to her flashes. APRIL glances at it in horror. JIA SHUYA controls her voice, walks quickly to the window, and closes it. She cries louder. She collapses on the ground leaning against the wall. Her lips tremble and she begins to sob. Her throat makes a continuous twitching sound.

> **APRIL**
>
> Where did he go? Didn't he bring the money today? What about tuition fees? What about living expenses?

JIA SHUYA has difficulty breathing, whimpering, and

even crying. APRIL stands, looking at the drawer
intently. The drawers are turned upside down. She
stretches out her arms and points at her mother
in hatred.

                    APRIL

          Do you know which casino he went to?
          I'll go find him!

A man, KONG FULAI in his fifties, rushes in.

                 KONG FULAI

               (In anger)
          APRIL, you'd better get out to make
          money and support yourself.

                    APRIL

          Dad, I'm still in college. You've
          already promised to support me.

                  JIA SHUYA

               (Voice has become hoarse)
          FULAI, you make us so miserable, why
          you not to gamble in casinos and work
          in a restaurant?

KONG FULAI picks up a teacup and throws it at JIA

SHUYA. JIA SHUYA screams and faints. KONG FULAI walks to the bed, and lifts the mattress, finding a wad of banknotes in his hand.

KONG FULAI

You don't fucking believe I can't win
it back.

KONG FULAI turns around and leaves. JIA SHUYA gets up.

JIA SHUYA

(Shouting hysterically)
We all lost; you can't take the money!
It's our life-saving money!

KONG FULAI kicks JIA SHUYA. She screams and falls to the ground. APRIL rushes over and hugs JIA SHUYA.

APRIL

Dad! Are you crazy? Are you going to
kill us?

KONG FULAI

(Eyes bloodshot, shouting)
Get out of here! Go away! I don't want

to see you again.

                    APRIL

Good! We will all be homeless. I am
your burden. I'm leaving, I'm looking
for a job, and I'm not going to study
anymore! You don't come to me again.

APRIL looks at her mother blankly. She picks up
her backpack, kicks a shoe at the door hard, opens
the door, and pushes the door back. She takes a
step forward, comes back, pulling the door back,
the door is blocked by the shoes and bounces back.
She doesn't look back and walks outside.

3. EXT. RIVERSIDE - SAME NIGHT

                    APRIL
                  (Cry loudly)
Woo hoo…

She walks into the darkness along the river. The
rain hits her face. On the riverside stands a
big drum-shaped stone. She cups her hands and
prays. She heard some squishing sounds. It was
HOMELESS 404, in his forties, walking, shouting
while pushing a shopping cart. (The scene freezes

on him pushing an old shopping cart filled with all his belongings.) He turns to a corner behind APRIL. APRIL turns around. She sees HOMELESS 404. His shopping cart and the sundries on it almost touch her. APRIL is scary. HOMELESS 404 shouts as he walks, his voice filled with frantic desperation and a cry for help.

                    HOMELESS 404

     It's raining, come on, come on. The
     sky is falling.

It is drizzling. APRIL walks quickly, and HOMELESS 404 is also walking behind. He pushes the shopping cart hard, constantly looking for the next possible shelter from the rain. APRIL steps into a dark and damp alleyway alone, trying to escape the rain. Suddenly, APRIL steps into the water on a low-lying surface, and her shoes get wet. She comes out quickly. HOMELESS 404 is beside her.

                    HOMELESS 404

     You stepped so accurately!

[Cut]

In the night and rain, the camera gradually blurs,

and the characters gradually disappear. The sound of the shopping cart hitting the pillar makes APRIL turn around in horror, and she quickens her pace and enters a supermarket. HOMELESS 404 finds a dry place at the entrance, takes out a worn-out piece of clothing from the shopping cart, and spreads it on the ground casually, he lays down, looking very satisfied.

                    HOMELESS 404
        I am the boss. I am 404. No mistake.

APRIL looks at him gently and tenderly.

4. INT. SUPERMARKET - LATE NIGHT

HOMELESS 404 sees APRIL leaning against the wall with her back all wet and walks over. He picks up the newspapers on the free newspaper shelf in the supermarket, handing one to APRIL. He tilts his head. He dries his hair with the newspaper. His hair stands up in tufts, looking a little funny like a clown. APRIL takes over the newspaper and reads job advertisements: urgently recruiting AI test experiencers, nursing home assistants, waterway maintenance workers, etc. She takes photos of these ads with her cellphone.

She leaves. Suddenly, the HOMELESS 404 utters a laugh ouch. APRIL steps on his foot. She quickly says sorry. He waves his hand to her, indicating not to worry.

5. I/E. TANG RESTAURANT - LATE MIDNIGHT

The streets are silent, with only faint lights. APRIL gets off the bus, carrying a backpack and looking tired. She stops in front of the TANG RESTAURANT. A one-story detached building with a stone-clad basement has a rich history. APRIL goes up the stone steps. She pushes the door lightly open. As soon as she enters the restaurant, the dim light casts strange shadows. The creaking sound of old wooden boards on the wall is chilling. She walks cautiously towards a corner; the shadows are frightening. Suddenly a mouse scuttles around the corner. She rushes past the corner. She suddenly screams. LI JIANSHE's voice comes from inside.

                         APRIL
                (Shocked, shouting softly)
            Oh my God! Who is it?

                      LI JIANSHE
                 (Voice from far away)
            Who woke the mouse?

A chill runs down APRIL's spine.

APRIL

(Whispering)

It's me, APRIL! No, no, mouse, oh my
God.

She quietly walks towards the door of MENG NING'S
room. Turning on the light. It is not MENG NING
lying on the bed, but LI JIANSHE, a man in his
fifties, with a bald and yellowish forehead with
a few sparse and greasy hairs on the back of his
head, lying on a simple single bed. His sleeping
eyes open.

LI JIANSHE

Hey, APRIL, are you coming to see me
or to my rat?

APRIL's eyes were widely open.

APRIL

I wanted to stay with sister MENG NING
for one night.

LI JIANSHE gets up, wearing shorts and a white
crew-neck sweatshirt.

LI JIANSHE

I am sleeping here now.

APRIL feels a wave of embarrassment in her heart and hesitates. She turns to leave.

LI JIANSHE

You sleep on the bed. I can sleep on the long stool.

APRIL

No, no, I'll just sit on the stool.

APRIL looks around and sits down. LI JIANSHE goes to the bathroom. APRIL hears his urinating. She walks out gently. It is dark outside. She is in a dilemma. She returns to the room. She sits on the stool again. LI JIANSHE comes over and pulls her.

LI JIANSHE

Go to bed and sleep. You don't have to be afraid. I won't even touch a piece of your hair.

MENG NING stands at the door for a movement, comes back. She smells alcohol. She sees LI JIANSHE holding APRIL's arm.

MENG NING

You bastard, you seduced APRIL. This
is a crematorium. Do you want to play
with fire?

LI JIANSHE

Why are you so angry?

MENG NING pushes APRIL with a straight face. APRIL
takes a few steps back and falls to the ground.

MENG NING

You are a holy girl, aren't you?

APRIL gets up and quietly wants to leave. But she
hesitates at the door.

LI JIANSHE

(To MENG NING)

The crematorium is for people like
you.

APRIL is afraid of the darkness outside. She has
no choice but to come in again.

APRIL

This was not a crematorium.

> **LI JIANSHE**
>
> Yes, it was. People were burned here in the past. XU MEILI bought it. It's cheap to open a restaurant here.

> **APRIL**
>
> Ah, no wonder the rats here are so scary.

The quiet restaurant was filled with dim light. APRIL is scared and faces a thick stonewall with a mournful face.

> **APRIL**
>
> (Talking to herself)
>
> Crematorium.

APRIL picks up a few napkins, studs them into her shoes, walks over, sits on a stool, leans her back against the counter, begins to check her laptop and sends her resume from the mobile phone.

6. INT. TANG RESTAURANT - NEXT DAY

APRIL begins to clear the tables and chairs, preparing to take a break. MENG NING and LI JIANSHE are talking. Behind the counter is the manager

and owner TANG JIN. His wife XU MEILI walks in.
LI JIANSHE quickly lowers his head.

XU MEILI

APRIL, you don't have a job. Why don't
you work here?

APRIL

Auntie XU, thank you. I don't want to
work in a restaurant all my life. I'm
looking for a job. But I can work here
in my spare time.

XU MEILI

You are so stubborn, no wonder your
dad blames you!

APRIL

I want to be myself. I wanted to be a
poet and a playwright as well.

XU MEILI

Alas, a chicken can become a flying
duck.

Manager TANG JIN comes over.

TANG JIN

Come play a mahjong game and get rid
of your anger.

APRIL reads emails on her cellphone and continues
to look for jobs. TANG JIN, XU MEILI, LI JIANSHE
and MENG NING sit around a table. LI JIANSHE takes
out a set of mahjong. Everyone puts their hands
on the mahjong to shuffle the cards. LI JIANSHE
distributes the cards to everyone. The atmosphere
becomes tense. Tang Jin draws the card.

TANG JIN
(Singing)
Come on - Wan, come on, Fa, come on -
fa.

MENG NING

Humph, I should have won.

MENG NING looks at Tang Jin. Tang Jin glances at
her. XU MEILI sees the two people's meeting eyes.
Face unhappy.

XU MEILI
(Shouting to Tang Jin)
What are you excited about?

APRIL sits in a corner preparing for the interview.
MENG NING collects all the banknotes from the
other three people.

                    MENG NING

               (Shouting to APRIL)
          You come here. I have to pee.

APRIL walks over, sits in MENG NING's seat.

                    LI JIANSHE
          She won the money and ran away.

7. INT. XU MEILI's HOME kitchen - AFTERNOON

XU MEILI is preparing a stir-fry, pouring oil
into the pot. The chili, ginger and garlic are
burning in the oil. JIA SHUYA stands next to her,
with tears in her eyes.

                    JIA SHUYA

               (Picks up the cooking spoon)
          Sister, let me help you.

                    XU MEILI
          You stay at my house first. I will find
          a nanny job for you.

JIA SHUYA

Sister, I am now almost homeless and
have to stay with you for a couple of
days. I think my life has come to an
end. That old man who hired me has
passed away.

8. Ext. SEAPARK - day

The seaside park is quiet and beautiful, with waves
lapping on the beach. The sun gradually sets. The
sky shows an orange-red afterglow. ELLIE, a young
AI company executive, a psychotherapist and a
script-writing enthusiast sits on a tree stump.
APRIL walks across the entire beach, coming to
sit with ELLIE quietly. ELLIE wears a pair of
glasses that have hidden lenses. ELLIE takes off
her glasses, and hands APRIL a pair of glasses
with black sides and black lenses.

ELLIE

Thank you for your application. You
will experience it through these AI
glasses.

ELLIE stands up, faces the sea, and opens her
arms.

ELLIE

(Loudly)

Fantasy will fill me until I die. I am
dead. My future is alive.

APRIL

(Smile)

You look like a hero. But I'm not.

ELLIE continues to keep her arms open.

ELLIE

(Laughing and shaking his head)

I'm more of an actor.

APRIL

Everyone in the world is an actor,
performing a show prepared by God.

ELLIE

(Affectionately)

Ah, the spring of AI will be like
spring flowers. Endless blooming is
everywhere.

APRIL

Am I experiencing AI,or is AI

experiencing me?

                    ELLIE

You'll be curious. You will know,
although the pay is not much.

9. EXT. INSIDE AI GLASSES - SEAPARK - DAY

APRIL sees the sea through her glasses.

                    APRIL

This virtual seaside scene is truly
beautiful.

                    ELLIE

Quietly.

                    APRIL
                  (Gently)
Yes, silence is like having wings,
everywhere. I have given you information
about my mother and me. Hey, could
this AI also help win money?

                    ELLIE

Yes, new experiences test. We work with
many companies, including gambling
ones. Life will change infinitely. The

virtual is not virtual, the real is
not real, and this is what the casino
needs most.

ELLIE takes off her glasses.

ELLIE

You should be in AI glasses now.

Through her glasses, APRIL sees a man walking
towards her from the bushes. AI ONION has purple
hair, a well-developed chest, a big belly, a big
beard on his mouth, and strong- arm muscles. He
carries a basket of roses on his back, holds
in his arms a baby-like AI JASMINE with yellow
hair and ear-length hair, wearing a close-fitting
white T-shirt and shorts. AI JASMINE's breasts
are mature and prominent like two small balls
on her chest flickering along with the walking
rhythm, very tempting. AI JASMINE is not wearing
shoes; her hands are slightly stretched forward.
She is holding a few roses and JASMINE flowers in
her hands. They all smile.

AI ONION

You won't believe our story. I am AI
Onion.

AI JASMINE

Hi, I was just born last night.

APRIL is confused, and a little scared. She points to the belly of the AI onion.

AI JASMINE

I was designed to come out of his belly.

AI JASMINE stretches out the rose in her hand to APRIL.

AI JASMINE
(Cheerfully)
This is for you.

APRIL
(Smiling happily)
Wow, thank you so much. Can you come down and walk?

AI JASMINE

I just pretend to be human and don't walk. I haven't learned to cry yet.

APRIL
Then you are so happy. Can't even cry.

10. INT. MEETING ROOM - AFTERNOON

More than a dozen staff members are scattered listening. A middle-aged Asian-looking woman stood in front, wearing a yellow gown, holding a mask in her hand, and giving a lecture and training on how to put on wearing protective clothing. She finishes. APRIL, wearing a mask, immediately goes over to ask her.

                         APRIL

        I am new here.

                         WOMAN

                    (To APRIL)

        Masks are useless.

APRIL opens her eyes wide with a panic. Old lady SOPHIE in a wheelchair rolls to the door to watch. When APRIL sees her, she immediately goes over and speaks into Sophie's ear. APRIL hugs her and whispers comforting words in her ear. APRIL's eyes are filled with tears. Sophie sits in a wheelchair and slowly moves toward the corridor, but then turns back and looks at APRIL.

11. INT. NURSING HOME - STAFF LUNCH ROOM - NOON

LISA, a fat female staff member with Asian appearance and fair skin, is dining. Two plates and two portions of food are on the table.

> APRIL
>
> (Smilingly)
>
> Wow, you eat two portions. That's pretty good.

> LISA
>
> (Suddenly angry)
>
> Are you blaming me for eating too much? That's none of your business.

> APRIL
>
> (Nervously and fearfully)
>
> Sorry, I didn't mean it. Please forgive me.

LISA immediately goes to the manager's office to complain. APRIL looks at LISA's back nervously.

12. INT. MANAGER'S OFFICE - NEXT MORNING

APRIL is waiting in the manager's office when the

manager comes in. She gestures for APRIL to sit
down, and she herself sits next to APRIL.

MANAGER

Do you know the language of nursing
homes? For example, talking about the
weather. She said you discriminate
against her.

APRIL

I didn't mean that.

MANAGER

I'd better suspend your job. You don't
have much working time anyway. You
don't want her to sue you.

13. INT. TANG RESTAURANT - AFTERNOON

MENG NING and APRIL sit opposite each other at
the table by the window. MENG NING is knitting
napkins.

MENG NING

Do you know? Your father has been
arrested.

APRIL

(Nervous and painful expression)
Ah?

MENG NING

You'd better live here!

APRIL

Live here? Terrible. Here is a burial
ground. I heard a youth hostel is very
cheap.

14. EXT. PARK - LAER THE DAY

APRIL leans against a tree, crying. She stops her
crying and looks at the recruitment information
on her mobile phone.

15. INT. INTERVIEW OFFICE - DAY

The two interviewers sit on one side of APRIL. She
smiles, trying to give them a kind and confident
feeling.

INTERVIEW MANAGER

As a science major, are you willing to
accept this cleanup work?

APRIL

(Smiling)

Yes, I am interested in an environmental
protection job.

INTERVIEW MANAGER

Why did you skip college? Fortunately,
we don't need to look at academic
qualifications. Junior high is fine.

APRIL

Thank you very much, please give me a
try, I need this job.

16. EXT. SMALL CREEK - DAY

APRIL and her two colleagues, LUKE and TERRY, are
in the water wearing waterproof suits with an
open-head design. In the creek, the salmons swim.
APRIL carries a charged rectangular electric box
making a thin squeaking sound on her back. She
stands in the water with a long pole in her hand
and the long pole is looking for salmon. She puts
the pole in the water to stun the salmon, puts the
fainted salmon into the bucket and then isolates
them on the other side of the water. After that,
they need to clean up the mud in the river and the

weeds on the riverside. APRIL looks serious and a little nervous.

APRIL

(Whisper to LUKE)

Do you promise not to kill the fish?

TERRY stands to the left of APRIL, carrying a bucket to hold the fish on Luke's net. APRIL watches the fish jumping in the water. Soon the bucket will be full. Then, APRIL picks up a small. The stunned fish is awake and is gently held in her arms.

APRIL

You are so beautiful! Don't be afraid, little one. We just make the river cleaner.

The sun shines on the water. APRIL's smile complements the clear water. Terry picks up a fish in the net where APRIL puts the salmon. The fish doesn't look very agile.

TERRY

(Yelling)

APRIL, come here quickly.

APRIL runs toward Terry. Terry points at the unconscious salmon.

TERRY

The fish seemed to be dead.

APRIL is horrified.

TERRY

I guess you don't have to come to work anymore.

APRIL looks at Terry pitifully and in surprise.

LUKE

The salmon are very active.

17.EXT. PARK - NEXT MORNING

APRIL leans against a tree, tears flowing silently, calls her mother.

APRIL

Mom, I have some sad news for you.

JIA SHUYA
(Nervous voice)
What? Are you OK?

APRIL

I was fired again.

(Beat)

Don't worry. I'm fine. How is dad?

JIA SHUYA

(Crying, very sad)

Your dad is going to court soon. The
lawyer asked for bail of $50,000.

APRIL

Fifty thousand? Where are we going to
get fifty thousand dollars? I'm going
to work in the restaurant today to see
if I can make more money.

JIA SHUYA

Mom is so incompetent, I'm sorry for
you.

APRIL turns off her phone, looks into the distance.
Repeats fifty thousand... Fifty thousand... She
sees people walking by on the road; some children's
hands are in the hands of their parents walking
towards a church. She watches silently, unable to
resist following a family into the church.

18. INT. TANG RESTAURANT - DAY

APRIL takes over MENG NING's shift, greeting customers at the restaurant's counter, and collecting payments. APRIL receives an order on the phone and walks to the kitchen to ask the chef to cook. She hears the restaurant owners uncle TANG JIN and LI JIANSHE saying her parents' names. She hides behind PING FENG and listens.

LI JIANSHE

(Shout softly)

My God! APRIL's mother thought casinos
were so profitable.

It's easy to force her husband to quit his job and go gambling. It's terrible.

TANG JIN

The same goes for engineers like this. If he is fired, he can still find another job! But he prefers to listen to his wife. Alas, no, if he has a calculating mind, doesn't he need the casino? Can he win by betting on a bag?

LI JIANSHE

A large part of human tragedy is caused

by greed.

The two of them laugh. APRIL enters through the door curtain. When they see APRIL, they shush each other.

19. INT. MIXED GENDER ROOM - EVENING

APRIL walks into the room carrying a small backpack and happens to meet Mike who just walks out of the public bathroom. Mike takes the initiative to say hi. APRIL sits on the edge of the bed, then walks to the public bathroom and finds a lot of dirty clothes on the floor. She comes back and approaches Mike.

> APRIL

Hey, are those clothes on the floor yours?

MIKE is lying on the bed. When he stands up, his pants fall down because he doesn't wear a belt, exposing his shorts. He lifts it up with his hand.

> MIKE
> (Embarrassingly)

I'll go get it right now.

APRIL

Are we the only two staying here
tonight?

MIKE

I live here every day.

APRIL

Oh, you don't have to go home.

MIKE

This is my home.

APRIL is silent.

MIKE

You're not here to travel? But no
one is. Coming now, only the new
coronavirus is flying everywhere.

APRIL

I came here to study when I was fourteen
and have stayed. I just lost my job,
come over here a bit.

MIKE

My parents just left this world and

went to heaven.

                    APRIL

                 (Eyes moist)
          Sorry, can I hug you?

Mike opens his arms and takes the initiative to
hug APRIL, but his pants fall again. At night,
two of them are lying on their two beds. APRIL
writes something in the notebook on his mobile
phone. APRIL stops and looks sideways at Mike,
who happens to be looking at her.

                    APRIL

          Do I look like a poet? But it's a
          secret.

                    MIKE

          It is normal for poets to be unemployed.
          Not everyone needs art.

                    APRIL

          Writing poetry is not for living.

APRIL puts on AI glasses.

20. EXT. INSIDE AI GLASSES - LAKESIDE - DAY

AI ONION's clothes are fancy, bright red pants and flowery shoes. A handkerchief is carried on the waist of the trousers. The top has a rose pattern on the chest, and a simple suspender is used to hang it around the neck. AI JASMINE starts running. She runs out, hugs and jumps on APRIL. She beams with joy when sees APRIL, affectionately. AI ONION picks up the handkerchief keeps spinning it, and gently lifts it into the air. He catches the throne handkerchief with his hand, but the handkerchief does not fly back to his hand. It lands on APRIL's head. April takes the handkerchief and makes a spinning motion with the handkerchief, but she can't do it well. She smiles, and so do the two AIs. AI JASMINE is carrying a basket of roses on her back. She is only a little below APRIL's waist. The way she stands on tiptoes makes APRIL smile.

                         APRIL
          Are you trying to wash away the dust
          from my soul?

AI JASMINE dances on tiptoes and draws circles on APRIL's chest with the rose in her hand. AI ONION looks at APRIL and sees a poem floating in the air in front of APRIL. AI ONION reads the sentence APRIL just wrote.

AI ONION

I always want to talk to you and enjoy a safe space.

AI JASMINE

We laugh, cry and hug her. Have you smelled my flowers yet?

AI JASMINE stands on tiptoe with her right foot, raises her left foot behind her, and opens her arms in a circular shape, as if hugging APRIL, who also opens her arms.

AI JASMINE[CONT'D]

A mask may not help protect me.

APRIL

Do you need a mask too?

AI ONION picks up the rose in its hand.

AI ONION

We need love.

> **APRIL**
>
> You make me feel alive.

21. INT. YOUTH HOSTEL - MIXED GENDER ROOM - EVENING

Mike gets up from the bed, walking over to read the words on APRIL's mobile phone. APRIL takes off his glasses.

> **MIKE**
>
> (Pointing to glasses)
>
> You make me feel lonely. You are experiencing glasses; I know who you are.

> **APRIL**
>
> Who am I?

APRIL gets up from the bed, goes to find a pill in his bag, and prepares to drink it with water from the water bottle in her bag.

> **APRIL[CONT'D]**
>
> This little pill helps me get some sleep. The doctor said something fdangerous to my body. If I can't fix it, I will face death all the time.

MIKE

Are you going to die? Let death retreat.

APRIL

You sound like you're speaking your lines.

Mike

You are beautiful. I will fall in love with you.

APRIL

Sensitive people are vulnerable. I once loved a liar.

APRIL looked at the moon outside the window.

MIKE

Is this anxiety?

APRIL

How do you know?

MIKE

I can figure out a lot of secrets, including making money. It's a secret.

22. EXT. ENTRANCE SLOPE OF THE CEMETERY PARK - DAY

A peaceful park nearby is in the sunshine. The wild apple trees are tall and straight. The sparse ripe apples are on the ground. APRIL picks up an apple. Mike walks under a crooked branch, stretches out his hand and jumps up to grab the apple on it. APRIL takes a photo of Mike picking apples. The photo is conveniently sent to Mike's cell phone.

> **MIKE**
> (Take a bite of an apple)
> Very sour. But this picture will bless me.

> **APRIL**
> (Looked around)
> Such a nice place, people thought it was a garden, but it's a cemetery park. You said your parents live here?

> **MIKE**
> Yes, they live here so I can often visit and look at them. Are you afraid?

> **APRIL**

Yes. What is scary is the living
people, not the dead.

She touches the old trunk and the rough bark.
Not far away is the coast. Mike points to a small
slope in the distance. The indigenous people there
donate their cemeteries to the Chinese.

APRIL

The terrain in that place is so low.
It could be hit by the sea at any time
and flooded.

MIKE

Yes, the Chinese who came in the early
days had no burial land after their
death.

APRIL

Death without a burial place is
terrible. No wonder my dad scolds my
mom like this.

MIKE

The sea waves also washed many graves
away.

APRIL takes out the AI eyeglasses from her bag and puts them on. April speaks in the direction of the cemetery in the distance.

APRIL

How are you doing? The seawater soaks in.

MIKE

These kinds of glasses are said to help relieve depression and also change the habits of living things.

APRIL

This is my trial; how do you know this?

MIKE

My guess. If something happens to me in the future that makes you unhappy, please forgive me. I hope you are happy.

APRIL

Well, thank you.

Gray birds chirp loudly in the surrounding trees.

Mike approaches APRIL's right side, stretches his left hand across her back to her left arm, holds it, and then moves to her left outer breast. He slowly hugs her left arm with his right hand in front of her and hugs her. His left hand continued to rub and tease her breasts. She feels a surge of heat coming out of her body and feels a little dazed.

                    APRIL

    My breath is all about you.

                    MIKE

         (In APRIL's ear.)
    You are sexy. You are charming.
    Tonight, can I sleep in your arms? So
    close, so close!

APRIL slightly breaks away from Mike's arm and moves a little away.

                    APRIL

    Look, it's going to rain.

MIKE raises APRIL's arms, and APRIL makes flying gestures.

APRIL

Wings, from now on, fly.

MIKE

Love from now on.

APRIL's cell phone rings.

APRIL

Hi, hello aunt.

XU MEILI

Can you come to the restaurant today?
I have something important to tell
you.

23. INT. TANG RESTAURANT - DAY

The restaurant is filled with the faint aroma of
cooking. The wooden tables and chairs exude traces
of time. APRIL opens the door. Mike follows. She
looks around. There were only a few scattered
customers in the restaurant. Mike orders a plate of
dumplings for himself and tries to use chopsticks,
but fails to pick up the dumplings, so he eats
them with his fingers. XU MEILI calls herself the
Yellow-faced woman. LI JIANSHE steps forward.

LI JIANSHE

Beautiful boss lady, your face is very
beautiful, it's still a little white
today. It's yellow inside.

XU MEILI

Oh, don't make fun of me.

APRIL

It was because the vitamin B my aunt
took was too active and it floated on
her face.

LI JIANSHE

I have no other intention but to thank
you for the wages you gave me today.

XU MEILI

You can pay your rent.

LI JIANSHE

Thanks. Now having my own place to
live is no longer a dream.

LI JIANSHE walks away and pats the cash in his
hand. XU MEILI calls APRIL to another place.

XU MEILI

Don't worry. I know it is inappropriate
not to pay you more. Here are two
hundred dollars for you.

(Beat)

XU MEILI

The government provides some subsidies.
The epidemic is serious.

APRIL

Aunt, do you know if my mother
instigated my dad to go gambling and
asked him to resign from his job?

XU MEILI

APRIL, there is a reason why people are
stupid sometimes. Your dad is having
trouble at work. He occasionally goes
to the casino and gets lucky to make a
lot of money. Your mother admired him
very much; Let him resign...

24. INT. YOUTH HOSTEL MIXED GENDER ROOM - EVENING

APRIL is lying on the bed, aching all over and

unable to get to sleep.

                    MIKE

Let's go to the casino and have some
fun.

                    APRIL

Mike, why do you still like casinos?
Aren't you afraid of losing money?

                    MIKE

APRIL, you can count on me.

                    APRIL

I remember you said that before. You
take away my suppressed emotions. It's
all figured out.

Mike immediately puts on his clothes, and APRIL
also gets up and puts on his coat.

                    APRIL

OK. Hope you have good luck today.

                    MIKE

You will, I promise.

APRIL

You have a mysterious weapon.

MIKE

Sneak on your power glasses.

APRIL

OK, my glasses are a product for my experiment job.

MIKE

Oh, what do you think?

APRIL

It's getting more and more amazing.

25. INT. CASINO - NIGHT

APRIL and MIKE stand at a card table and watch, with anticipation and nervousness on their faces. The mood also fluctuates with every card turned over. The surrounding gamblers make various praises and exclamations. Some people are beaming with joy, while others are eclipsed.

APRIL

(To Mike's ear)

If I win money, I can continue to stay in the hostel or I will sleep on the street. Mike, if you win big money, you can buy a house.

MIKE

(Smiles)

My parents left me a big House. I sold it. I just want to live in that Youth Hostel.

APRIL

(With tears in eyes)

I want a room to write my poems. Is there any other way I can make money right away? I have no unemployment insurance. I send out resumes every day.

MIKE

Delicacy and sensitivity are the qualities of a poet that make you beautiful and vulnerable.

Mike took out two twenty-dollar bills from his pocket.

MIKE [CONT'D]

Don't worry. I'm familiar with how to
win money in casinos.

APRIL

Thanks. I will buy the chips myself.

APRIL and Mike are sitting at the roulette table,
watching the ball roll on the roulette wheel.

MIKE

Casinos   are   always   filled   with
uncertainty and excitement.

APRIL

(Holding chips)

You said it's pure luck.

APRIL puts on his glasses.

26. EXT. INSIDE AI GLASSES SEAPARK - DAY

Sea waves appear in the glasses, so it feels like
surfing or swimming instead of gambling. Two AIs
appear, one must be AI ONION with an onion on his
head, and the one with a rose on her head must be
AI JASMINE. They accompany APRIL for a walk on

the beach.

                        AI JASMINE
I became an adult as soon as I was
born. So, I can come to the casino.

                         APRIL
              (Pointing to the back)
Mike and I come here to gamble,
otherwise I won't have a place to live.

                        AI JASMINE
Heck, none of us are trained to
gamble, Mike's AI is trained. His AI
is guaranteed to win.

                         APRIL
Wow.

                        AI ONION
Yes, it's a pity that we are not. If
we were, you would earn it.

27.INT.CASINO - NIGHT LATER

APRIL decides to try her luck at roulette.

APRIL

(With a smile to Mike)

I chose No. 11, 1 to accompany 1. Like

you are accompanying me.

The ball is released and rolls on the roulette wheel, projecting nervous light and shadow. Dancing along the edge of the roulette wheel, the air is temporarily filled with suspense. APRIL holds her breath and watches the ball lose power and finally almost stop.

MIKE

(Cheers)

Wow, hit! Lucky number!

APRIL smiles and makes a high-five with Mike.

APRIL

(Glad)

Bingo! We won!

MIKE

(Slapping the table excitedly)

Marvelous! Finally got some good luck.

APRIL looks calm but her heart beats faster. Win

again. They cheer. Mike adds all the winnings to
the chips. Win again.

> MIKE
>
> (Laughed)
>
> The probability of winning with the
> same number three times is very low.

> APRIL
>
> Thanks. Let's go. Unpredictable world.

> MIKE
>
> You haven't lost yet. You can still
> play.

> APRIL
>
> I stopped playing because I was afraid
> that I might lose.

> MIKE
>
> Don't you have the joy of adventure?

> APRIL
>
> I'm afraid the trap will be activated.

> MIKE
>
> There are some traps.

28. INT. YOUTH HOSTEL MIXED GENDER ROOM - NIGHT
LATER

A sudden loud explosion and dazzling flash of light scared APRIL to the point where she sits up. She grabs her backpack and prepares to run outside.

APRIL

Earthquake.

MIKE grabs her and stops her from running outside. MIKE points out the window, which is stained red with sparks.

MIKE

It's dangerous out there.

Under the bright lights of the sky, a large group of marchers come to the streets. Some people shout to express their dissatisfaction with the new coronavirus measures and quarantine policies, and some oppose racial discrimination. Various emotions break out together. They wave flags, shout slogans, and angrily walk toward businesses to vent their anger. The sound of shop windows and doors being smashed is particularly jarring in the silence after the night's explosions. Someone is burning something. The plane was hovering in the sky nearby, and APRIL is stunned by this unexpected situation.

                          APRIL
                        (Panicked)
        Oh, my gosh! What's going on?

APRIL looks around nervously.

                          MIKE
        Look, someone is shouting and yelling
        on the rooftop opposite. Shouting is
        like crazy yell! He looked like he was
        about to jump off!

                          APRIL
                       (At a loss)
        Look, the man is dancing, as if he
        has completely lost control. Almost
        fell off the roof. Ah, he seems to be
        my father.

The man dancing on the roof is shouting like crazy! He is extremely emotional. Suddenly, he seems to lose his balance and fall... APRIL is trembling all over and calls the emergency phone.

> MIKE
> (Hugging APRIL)
Your hands are shaking, and I'm dialing, too.

29. INT. TANG RESTAURANT - DAY

APRIL watches ELLIE eating dumplings.

> ELLIE
You said the person who fell from the roof was your father?

> APRIL
Well, it's my entire fault. Fortunately, a tree supported him. I'm very anxious now. My illness may have returned.

> ELLIE
You can talk to the AI. They are training and trying to experience human feelings.

> APRIL
Good.

> ELLIE

I suggest you go to my place and do Transcranial Magnetic Stimulation (TMS) treatment.

                    APRIL

That costs a lot of money. I don't have that much money to do it. Can AI glasses help me make money?

                    ELLIE

That's the casino's AI. It is specially customized for the casino. It cost a lot of money.

                    APRIL

Is that Mike's AI?

                    ELLIE

Yes, but it is not the same system as ours. Ours helps people find spiritual comfort.

                    MIKE (V.O)

Only Mike's AI can help you.

30. I/E. APRIL'S HOME - EVENING

JIA SHUYA washes her hands repeatedly. She locks the door and goes back to wipe the door lock with alcohol again and again. Then She goes back to the bedroom and lies down on the bed. The computer automatically turns on the screen. JIA SHUYA's own face appears on the screen. She calls on her mobile phone, and the echo on the phone is that she can't get through. APRIL sits at the door and calls her mother on her phone.

APRIL

Why do you lock the door?

JIA SHUYA quickly walks to the door. After opening the door, JIA SHUYA takes a few steps back, feeling happy and sad when she sees her daughter.

JIA SHUYA

(Surprise)

Are you back and drinking?

APRIL

You don't have to worry about me.

APRIL walks directly to the bedroom, and her mother stops her.

JIA SHUYA

(Pointing to the open computer screen)
Why are you doing this to me, making
me talk to AI?

APRIL

Because you have psychological
anxiety, talk to AI and don't convey
your anxiety to me. You can also make
money.

JIA SHUYA

If you wander around every day, nothing
good will come of it.

APRIL

I just want to make you angry because
you asked dad to gamble.

JIA SHUYA

He used to win money every time. He
gambles money to support you too. For
your sake, you used to use his gambling
money!

APRIL

The result now is what you designed!

So, I hate you.

                    JIA SHUYA

Why are you like this? What did I do
wrong? Does he make money to support
us?

                    APRIL

You must accept that this is how your
daughter is.

                    JIA SHUYA

How is your job search going?

                    APRIL

I've searched them all, but there's no
place for me.

                    JIA SHUYA

I have to leave here in a few days.
Your uncle Tang Jin lost the bet, real
estate, and half the restaurants.

APRIL doesn't finish listening and she walks out.

31. INT. YOUTH HOSTEL - MIXED GENDER ROOM - EVENING

                    MIKE

(Talking to himself)

Where has she gone? The bag is not there either.

He asks the front desk.

MIKE

Has APRIL checked out?

FRONT DESK

Yes.

32. EXT. CITY STREET - NIGHT

APRIL walks out and takes a few more steps to stop her crying. She walks to the road again, and calls Mike. Mike doesn't answer. She puts on one of her headphones and continues walking along the road. She thinks of her glasses and puts them on.

33. EXT. INSIDE AI GLASSES - LAKESIDE - NIGHY

APRIL enters the glasses, with AI ONION and AI JASMINE to her left and right, walking together. In the dark, they are like people who are lost, looking for the right direction. They walk in a hurry as if someone is chasing them. Rain is hitting the roofs of the cars parked on the roadside. There is a sound in the air.

APRIL

I am dead, who are you, I am desperate, and who are you?

AI ONION

Death is officially here, that feeling.

AI JASMINE

So realistic.

APRIL stops and goes to the grass by the roadside to blow his nose.

AI ONION

It looked like she was in extreme pain, sitting in pain. The windmill came in a carriage.

AI JASMINE

She could only lie down and lie down.

APRIL's phone vibrates; it is Mike's voice. The sound of cell phone calls.

MIKE

How are you? Baby.

APRIL

Uh-huh---

APRIL looks around and sees that there is no one around. She walks to a small bush under a streetlamp. She starts crying.

MIKE

What's wrong?

APRIL

Why am I so miserable, so miserable?

MIKE

It's okay, baby.

APRIL

(Crying while blowing his nose)
Why am I so miserable, why am I
so miserable, everything I have.
My classmates all have salaries of
hundreds of thousands and hundreds of
thousands, and they are all married.
I have no school, no friends, no job,

and no money. My father originally
quit his job to gamble for my mother
and me. He was the one who casino
winnings gave us life. Maybe I blamed
my dad wrongly. I am still in the NEET
group. not in employment, education or
training, I'm ashamed.

MIKE

You are good; you have at least one
friend, no shame in being a NEET. Tell
me, did you fight?

There is a drizzle in the sky, and the cold
raindrops sprinkle on her face, combining with
the tears in her eyes to form a blurry picture.

APRIL

My father beat me when I was little.
He tied me up after drinking. On the
tree, hit me with a belt.

She looks around and sees the flashing car security
system work lights in the cars parked next to the
road.

Cold rain curtains on the road. Swinging in the

wind, as helpless as APRIL, and falling heavily and fragilely on her face, expressing her feelings together with her tears. She bursts into tears uncontrollably.

APRIL looks back in horror. What seems like a low moan, a low groan, a deep sense of oppression, or a sound like a knock suddenly appears, and a sense of terror suddenly strikes her. She looks back now in the car, starts to run away, and then wants to look back to confirm whether anyone is sitting in the car, but the rain hits the roof of the car.

> MIKE
> (Voice on the phone)
> The sun is coming out.

> APRIL
> I didn't dare to go out, I just approached death in the night.

Some low-frequency vibrations penetrate her deep heartbeat. She runs across the street and goes to the public stairs next to a house, with streetlights high above her.

> MIKE

> Let's continue; please tell me where
> you are now. Is it safe?

Another sound that sounds like a person venting their breath and like a distorted tone, causing abnormal or unnatural hearing.

                         MIKE
> Don't worry, baby, you are not alone.

APRIL sobs and looks around in horror, as if the whole world is against her.

34. INT. CASINO - NIGHT

In the dark corner of the casino, APRIL is sleeping soundly against a hidden corner. Wearing glasses, she enjoys a peaceful sleep while bathing in the dim casino lights. The various sounds of the casino seem to be isolated, and only a faint light penetrates the darkness of the night.

Suddenly, two figures stand out from the din of the casino. These two figures are AI ONION and AI JASMINE. They walk to APRIL's side.

                      AI ONION

                    (Quietly)
          Look, APRIL found peace in this dark
          corner.

                        AI JASMINE
               She is like a child.

     AI JASMINE put her fingers on April's forehead.

                        AI JASMINE
               See, she has a poem in her head.

     They decide to read in the air in front of APRIL.
     They sit on the ground in front of APRIL.

                        AI JASMINE
                    (Reading gently)
               The hustle and bustle of the casino
               time strands.

     They continue to browse the air in front of APRIL,
     as if in a virtual and quiet poetic space, talking
     to the girl's soul. In this casino, poetry and
     dreams seem to have their own place. APRIL and AI
     ONION and AI JASMINE are reading APRIL's poems.

     [Flashback]

On a rainy night, APRIL is walking in the rain with two AIs wearing glasses. There was a sound in the air.

72

> **APRIL**
>
> I ran away. The pain is so lonely.

> **AI ONION**
>
> There were only tears. Everyone was asleep.

> **APRIL**
>
> It suddenly occurred to me that there were scary people sitting inside.

> **AI JASMINE**
>
> I'm the same as everyone else.

> **APRIL**
>
> I started running, this was not death, I was still alive.

APRIL continues to sleep.

35. INT. CASINO - EARLY MORNING

MIKE looks around anxiously in the casino, with

a worried expression on his face. He finds APRIL curls up alone in the corner, sleeping quietly. MIKE walks up to APRIL and gently shakes her shoulders.

> **MIKE**
>
> APRIL, wake up. It's cold here.

APRIL slowly opens his eyes and looks at Mike in confusion.

> **MIKE**
> (Gently)
> It's me, APRIL. Why did you fall asleep here?

> **APRIL**
> (Slightly stunned)
> I... I won some money here. Tired and nowhere to go.

APRIL slowly sits up from the corner.

> **MIKE**
> (Slightly worried)
> Are you OK? Something seems wrong with you.

APRIL

(Smile)

It's okay; I can continue to do TMS
treatment.

MIKE

TMS treatment?

APRIL

It is a method of treating depression.

When MIKE hears APRIL mention depression, a flash
of shock and concern flash in his eyes.

36. INT. TMS ROOM - DAY

In a comfortable treatment room, ELLIE communicates
with APRIL, explaining the treatment process and
possible feelings. APRIL sits on the treatment
chair, the TMS device is gently fixed on her head,
and the guide coil is close to her forehead. Warm
lighting and soothing music create a peaceful
atmosphere in the room.

ELLIE

Are you feeling, okay? There may be a slight

irritation.

The TMS device emits intermittent magnetic pulses, which are transmitted to APRIL's cerebral cortex. APRIL closes her eyes gently with a subtle vibration.

                    ELLIE
        This is a normal feeling. This
        stimulation can help improve symptoms
        of depression.

                    APRIL
            (Smiling slightly)
        This feeling makes me feel lighter.

                    ELLIE
        That's fine, you just need to relax and
        let the treatment take effect.

APRIL closes her eyes, takes a deep breath, and looks very relaxed.

                    ELLIE
        You did very well. Your AI glasses can
        accompany you. Hope that will help.

At the front desk, APRIL takes out 400 dollars to

pay.

                    APRIL

Could you please give me a discount?

                 FRONT LINER

We've given you a 5% discount for
paying in cash.

37.INT. APRIL'S HOME - EVENING

JIA SHUYA is lying in the quilt. There are clothes
everywhere in the messy room. She is calling her
husband KONG FULAI.

                 KONG FULAI

How is APRIL doing lately?

                  JIA SHUYA

              (Voice on the phone)

She will never come to me except for
money.

                 KONG FULAI

Is she still willing to work in the
restaurant?

                  JIA SHUYA

I have no idea. Ask her yourself.

KONG FULAI

What do you do as a mother?

38. INT. TANG RESTAURANT - EVENING

APRIL stands leaning against the restaurant's cluttered staff room to answer her mother's call. (Voice on the phone)

JIA SHUYA

Your dad wants to talk to you.

APRIL

You complained to him again. I can't see him all year round, do you want to blame me?

LI JIANSHE comes in and calls APRIL loudly.

JIA SHUYA

(Phone sound)

Okay, okay, no more.

APRIL puts away the phone. When LI JIANSHE sees that APRIL finishes the call, he shouts.

> LI JIANSHE

APRIL, let's go and find the boss. He said that the restaurant would be closed due to poor business.

39. EXT. TANG RESTAURANT - EVENING LATER

The sky is particularly transparent, and the moon is very round. LI JIANSHE takes out two cigarettes and hands one to APRIL. He takes out his lighter and lit one, and then offers the lit one to light APRIL's cigarette. APRIL takes the cigarette and sends it back.

> APRIL

Thank you, I don't smoke.

> LI JIANSHE

You can save a lot of money. Cigarettes are too expensive here.

> APRIL

Um.

> LI JIANSHE

Why do work here? Sorry to ask more.

APRIL

It was Aunt MEILI who asked me to help. Most are volunteers.

LI JIANSHE

This is not a charity, why is it a volunteer?

APRIL

I was embarrassed to ask for money before. But I will get paid.

LI JIANSHE

It's okay to ask for money. It is said that your dad is an engineer and makes a lot of money.

APRIL

Um.

LI JIANSHE blows out smoke and seems to enjoy this kind of life.

LI JIANSHE

Life is like a dream. It's gambling. I like gambling, life is like a dream.

MENG NING is listening. She approaches them directly and takes up the conversation.

> MENG NING
>
> How to say this?

> APRIL
>
> I am very afraid of gambling and not winning.

> MENG NING
>
> Afraid of losing, she is afraid of taking off her underwear and baring her buttocks.

> LI JIANSHE
>
> It's different here.

> MENG NING
>
> Free pick-up and drop-off, free buffet. Yeah?

> LI JIANSHE
>
> Some people just play slot machines and buy a house. Stimulate! Luck.

40. INT. TANG RESTAURANT - AFTERNOON

APRIL, LI JIANSHE and the other guys are all busy working. The customers gradually disperse and politely say goodbye to them. LI JIANSHE clears the table, picks up the dollar bills, and stuffs them into his pocket. Currently, another guest is coming. LI JIANSHE asks MENG NING to take charge. In LI JIANSHE's view, although MENG NING is still in her thirties, she is plump and charming, eloquent, and liked by everyone. She is also the distant niece of the landlady.

LI JIANSHE

MENG NING, come to help.

LI JIANSHE shouts twice, and when he sees that MENG NING is not there, he enters the kitchen. When he sees that MENG NING is still not there, he turns around and asks APRIL. APRIL sees that LI JIANSHE's eyes are a little strange and says nothing. APRIL opens the door and investigates the kitchen, where she sees the fat and bald boss Tang Jin coming. The boss's face is a bit ugly, especially his eyes. APRIL is a little afraid of him and takes a few steps back. She hears TANG JIN talking. LI JIANSHE only hears XU MEILI coming from outside, followed by several people.

Including Mike who comes over to eat dumplings.

XU MEILI

(Called to guests)
Sorry, sir, it's time to get off work.

MIKE

(Pointing to the timetable posted on the door)
Madam, it is not right.

XU MEILI

Under special circumstances, it will
be closed early.

The guest and Mike look up at the yellow-faced
woman strangely.

MIKE

(Quietly)
Who is this woman?

LI JIANSHE

(Quietly)
Boss lady, something is going on.

APRIL and LI JIANSHE watch the yellow-faced
proprietress XU MEILI and two strong men enter

the back kitchen. They look at each other in
horror and sit at a table. There are sounds of
bowls being thrown and pots being knocked. The
boss is beaten until he begs.

XU MEILI

(Viciously)

You find that slut.

TANG JIN

No such thing, you wronged me!

XU MEILI

Did I wrong you? How much did you give
her?

TANG JIN

No, not a penny.

XU MEILI

Sign it! Give up property rights.

Boss Tang Jin seems to be suffocated. Then he cries
out "wow". LI JIANSHE hears it.

LI JIANSHE

Fortunately,   he   didn't   die,   but

strangulation would have killed someone.

                    MIKE

What's wrong? Silent? dead?

                 LI JIANSHE

No way. Don't look!

APRIL is frightening. She wants to go in and have a look, but Mike holds her back.

                    MIKE

It will be dangerous for you to go in!

                   APRIL

She is my aunt!

                    MIKE

Ah, what should I do if someone is dead inside? First...call the police!

                 LI JIANSHE

Wait, wait.

As Mike, APRIL and LI JIANSHE listen, there is a loud closing sound from the back door.

LI JIANSHE

Gone! They're gone. It's a good thing
that MENG NING escaped, otherwise...

Boss Tang Jin stumbles out and uses a white kitchen
towel to press the bleeding wound on his head. LI
JIANSHE hurriedly gets up and goes to help Tang
Jin.

TANG JIN

Finished.

APRIL

Uncle, where is my aunt?

BOSS TANG JIN

Your aunt ran away with someone!

APRIL

How did that happen? I do not believe
it.

TANG JIN

Snort! Go ask her!

LI JIANSHE

Alas, how could you be so careless when you got this? Money can solve things, small things!

TANG JIN

Let's close the door for two days!

41.INT.YOUTH HOSTEL - MIXED GENDER ROOM - DAY

Mike and APRIL are lying on the same bed respectively.

MIKE

I know your glasses. It's a secret.

APRIL

Are you the mysterious assistant?

MIKE

We can share it once but don't tell anyone.

42.INT.YOUTH HOSTEL - MIXED GENDER ROOM - DAY

The outer door suddenly opens, and a new female resident arrives. A thin scarf is wrapped around the mouth area of the face.

> **MENG NING**
>
> You should stay away from me. I might get COVID-19. My name is MENG NING, peaceful Ning. Dream of peace. Dream!

APRIL hears the sound and quickly puts the mask on. Take off the glasses and put them in her bag. MENG NING dials a phone number, and shouts into the phone.

> **MENG NING**
>
> They all asked me if I had COVID-19. I'm dead.

> **MIKE**
>
> Are you sure your bed is here?

> **MENG NING**
>
> (Retreat to the door of the room and
>   look at the door NUMBER)
> Oh, it's the opposite side.

Waiting for MENG NING to leave, APRIL opens her eyes wide and is shocked.

43. INT. YOUTH HOSTEL - PUBLIC KITCHEN ROOM - DAY

Mike is using the computer, and MENG NING comes
over quietly and gets behind Mike. She sees Mike
and JIA SHUYA's heads appear on Mike's computer
screen. Mike quickly pushes the laptop screen
down but doesn't close it completely. MENG NING
leaves quickly.

> ### MIKE
>
> Is it okay to peek into other people's
> stuff? Hey, stop it! Who are you?

> ### MENG NING
>
> No, answer me first, who are you? How did
> APRIL's mom shows up on your computer?

> ### MIKE
>
> Oh my god, what did you see?

> ### MENG NING
>
> You! Isn't that her face?

> ### MIKE
>
> It's so cold. I think you've got the
> wrong person.

44.INT. APRIL'S HOME - DAY

JIA SHUYA sits in front of the computer. When she opens her hand, the computer automatically turns on the screen. Blog's cartoon face appears on the screen. This guy's face looks like Mike's.

JIA SHUYA

Please tell me first who you are. I'm worried about my daughter.

BLOG POST

I'm just a helper in developing programs and gathering storylines for scripts.

A beautifully crafted golden key appears on the screen. It has beautiful carvings of seashells and waves.

BLOG POST

Mrs. JIA, there is no use worrying. Please look at the key. The story inside will be revealed under its guidance.

JIA SHUYA

This is no ordinary key; it's like a key waiting to be revealed mystery.

The light from the computer screen stretches into the space in front of and above JIA SHUYA, emitting colorful dense lights. The rays surround JIA SHUYA like a cylinder from top to bottom. To the beat of the music, JIA SHUYA follows. Nod to the music and move her body naturally.

                    JIA SHUYA
          (Speaking while stepping to the beat)
          I think about when my daughter was
          born.

[Flashback]

45. EXT. SEAPARK - DAY

The sun shines on the earth, casting bright sunlight. The soft sand of the beach extends to the seaside, mixing with some shells and seaweed. JIA SHUYA picks up some seaweed from the beach. She sits down on the blanket. APRIL sits on the blanket and listens to music.

                    APRIL
        (Pointing to the seaweed in her mother's hand)
          These seaweeds are poisonous and

cannot be eaten.

JIA SHUYA quickly throws away the things in her hands.

                    JIA SHUYA

What poison? You are worried about anything. You should get a doctorate.

                     APRIL

Poison caused by sea pollution. Does dad have enough money to support my education?

                    JIA SHUYA

He won some money at the casino, but don't imitate him. He has a talent for this.

[Flashback]

46. INT. TANG RESTAURANT - DAY

JIA SHUYA wears work clothes, lying on a dirty bench and calling her husband. Voices on the phone.

KONG FULAI

Two thousand dollars have been sent.

JIA SHUYA

(Blaming voice)

Just two thousand? Didn't you agree to

three thousand? It's been four months,

where is the money?

KONG FULAI

I'm feeling a bit unlucky.

JIA SHUYA's hand holding her chin gets tired,
so she lies on her side and snorts on the phone,
expressing her anger.

KONG FULAI

(Voice on the phone, reproaching)

The creditor pressed for repayment,

and even I had to sell my kidney to

collect the 20,000 dollars, but no. I

want to pay off the debt. I wanted to

come over, where are you? If I am not

familiar with the casino, I will suffer

a loss.

JIA SHUYA

Come here quickly. APRIL is still
rebellious, and she has no money. I
can't stand it.

KONG FULAI

If I come and I can't make money
gambling, who will support this family?

[Flashback]

47. INT. APRIL'S HOME - DAY

APRIL comes back from school, opens the door, and
sees the open suitcases on the ground.

APRIL

Dad is back.

KONG FULAI finds his cup with the tea leaves. JIA
SHUYA is busy. She quickly walks over to pick up
the kettle and fills it with water. KONG FULAI sits
down on the stool at the dining table. JIA SHUYA
lets the water boil in the kettle and sits on the
sofa.

KONG FULAI

How is APRIL doing?

JIA SHUYA

You're back, talk to her.

Hearing his wife talking, he immediately becomes
unhappy, and her voice becomes louder and angrier.

KONG FULAI

You are a mother! I haven't seen what
you have done to help her.

JIA SHUYA

All the time, I worried about the money
more than anything else.

KONG FULAI suddenly becomes furious. His face
turns to ocher; his eyes open angrily.

KONG FULAI

(Loud)

Shut up! I never vent my stress to
you, but you vent your anxiety to me?
I should disappear in front of you!

JIA SHUYA

I'm telling you the truth.

KONG FULAI grabs the vacuum cleaner beside him

raises it above his head, and approaches JIA SHUYA, threatening to hit her. APRIL walks in.

KONG FULAI

You treated me with your stupid anxiety, you should reflect on yourself. What have you been doing? I'm already fed up. You'd better not irritate me.

KONG FULAI [CONT'D]

(Pointing to the window)

Believe me, you b... I just throw you out the window if you don't shut up.

JIA SHUYA

(Crazy)

I know what you will do. Grab my hair and kick my body. You can be violent to me anytime, anywhere.

JIA SHUYA sat motionless.

JIA SHUYA[CONT'D]

You know what you have done to my daughter, and me is domestic violence. You physically abuse us. That's the devil's miens.

KONG FULAI completely loses control of his anger, and he throws the vacuum cleaner at his wife. JIA SHUYA dodges it. The vacuum cleaner hit APRIL's arms and knocked the trashcan over and trash was now all over the floor APRIL was painful and cried.

                    APRIL

You! Can you stop? You make me sick!

APRIL points at the trashcan and cries.

48.INT.YOUTH HOSTEL - RESTROOM - DAY

MENG NING peeps from her room and sees APRIL holding her stomach and walking to the toilet. MENG NING went over and waited for APRIL to come out. Soon APRIL opens the toilet door and is surprised that MENG NING stands beside.

                MENG NING

I want to talk to you. Tell me, who is
the guy with you?

                    APRIL

Who? Mike? He is a good man.

MENG NING

Let's move somewhere else. Your roommate seems odd. He's the kind of man with a lot of mysteries.

APRIL

The new crown is blowing in the sky and on the ground. Everyone's life and death are unknown.

MENG NING

Let me tell you, a simple person like you, never be trapped by that guy. Leave your poems in the bright moonlight.

MENG NING turns around, walks out of the toilet.

MENG NING (CONTINUE)

Look up at the bright moon and look down at your hometown.

APRIL also walks out of the toilet.

APRIL

I would not call my hometown a bright moon.

> **MENG NING**
>
> I heard that your classmate from our hometown jumped off the building and died.

> **APRIL**
>
> I'm going to his memorial service tomorrow.

49. INT. CEMETERY BUILDING - DAY

Five people with masks at the cemetery funeral home to say farewell to the dead. APRIL looks sad. APRIL walks out of the funeral home and sees job recruitment info on the wall: Urgently hiring cemetery store cashier. Working hours: 11 pm to 6:30 am. APRIL walks to the nearby store and asks for the job requirements.

> **APRIL**
>
> Can I work here? I have a clean criminal record for working in a nursing home.

50. INT.YOUTH HOSTEL - MIXED GENDER ROOM - DAY

APRIL looks out of the window, seeing the empty

streets.

                         APRIL

    Starting tomorrow, I will go to the
    cemetery for cremation work from
    midnight to morning. I don't need a
    place to sleep now.

                         MIKE

    You said you were interested in a
    computer science technical writing
    career. You have a talent for writing.

                         APRIL

    I urgently need money to pay rent and
    food.

                         MIKE

    I'll see if I can help you.

After Mike leaves, A MAN in his forties smelling
alcohol walks in with a bag on his back. He puts
his backpack on the bed and turns around to see
APRIL walking into the room after him.

                         MAN

    How did you get into my room?

APRIL

This is my room.

MAN

Shut up.

The man suddenly kicks APRIL's female private parts under her belly.

MAN

(Mutter)

You whore.

APRIL feels great pain. The man grabs the AI glasses on APRIL's bed and puts them on his head, falling on the bed. The man opens his eyes again.

MAN

What are you talking about, are you interested in me? Come, come, and hurry up.

With his two bloody eyes wide open, he stands up unsteadily and tries to hug her with both arms. She forcefully breaks away, picks up her bag, grabs his glasses, and runs out to the lobby with tears in her eyes. APRIL goes to the front desk.

APRIL

Check me out!

APRIL walks out of the youth hostel carrying a backpack.

51. INT. CEMETERY STORE - DAY

It is APRIL's first day work. People line up for their memorial service. APRIL wears a mask and coughs lightly. Immediately people nearby turn their heads to look. The atmosphere is tense, as if everyone is infected with the coronavirus. She sees a lady holding a photo of a familiar person. The lady who holds the photo is Sophie's daughter LUNA. Luna is in tears. APRIL approaches Luna.

APRIL

(To Luna)

Sorry, Sophie. May your soul rest in peace.

LUNA

Are you APRIL? My mother has always wanted to see you again.

APRIL

Sorry, visits are not allowed.

52.EXT. CEMETERY STORE - EARLY MORNING

APRIL gets off work after a long night's work.

                    LUNA
          This is a pair of earrings left by my
          mother. There are two hundred dollars
          in the red envelope; she hopes to help
          you find a place where you can write
          poems.

                    APRIL
          I'm very grateful and touched, but
          these should belong to you

                    LUNA
          This is her wish. Thank you for your
          acceptance.

Sophie's daughter leaves. APRIL looks at the
street. She sees a man lying on the ground, and
there seem to be no signs of life. APRIL walks
over quickly. Someone else approaches. APRIL
takes out his cell phone to call the police. The

police come soon.

                        POLICE

    He died.

Everyone wears masks. APRIL looks around. The
dead man on the ground emits a bad smell, which
makes APRIL sick. APRIL takes out her AI glasses
from her bag and puts them on.

53.EXT. INSIDE AI GLASSES - LAKESIDE - DAY

APRIL enters the glasses. Salmon are floating in
a nearby stream. Some dead salmons are on the
shore. AI onion dressed in leaves. AI JASMINE
dresses in grass, carrying a basket of grass on
her back. As before, she rushes towards APRIL as
soon as she sees her.

                    AI JASMINE

    COVID-19 fell in love with my roses
    and jasmines.

                        APRIL

    So, you only have grass today?

                    AI JASMINE

Yes, you don't want to talk to a virus.

APRIL

I wanted to tell them that I couldn't do the work at the crematorium either. So sad.

AI ONION

The virus has already placed a bet.

APRIL

But I need to work.

AI ONION

I see humans entering casinos.

AI JASMINE

Many people's lives and deaths are unknown.

APRIL

Do you know how to save humanity? Do you know when I will die?

AI JASMINE

If you don't know death, how can you know life? I hope I can answer your question.

AI ONION

In the past, humans bet on horse racing, but now they bet on their own real-life experiences.

54. INT. YOUTH HOSTEL MIXED GENDER ROOM - EVENING

The room is dimly lit, with only a faint light coming from the dusty windows. Mike moves the sleeping man's shoulders.

MIKE

Did you hit APRIL?

MAN

Oh, bah.

The man spats at Mike, and the saliva lands on Mike's mask. The man stands up and then falls to the ground. Mike throws away the mask, washes his face, goes to the kitchen to turn on the computer, operates his program, and finds clues to APRIL.

IN THE KITCHEN

MENG NING walks over and coughs a few times.

MENG NING

The world is so small; I have to see
you again.

Mike quickly puts on his mask.

MIKE

Tell me who you are.

MENG NING

I can't wait to know who you are.

MIKE

I ate dumplings in the restaurant. You
are Miss MENG.

Mike ignores MENG NING again and immerses himself
in searching for APRIL on his computer. After a
while, a photo of APRIL picking apples for him
appears.

[FLASHBACK]

The scene shifts to the past. MIKE and APRIL pick up

apples that fall on the grass with laughers. MIKE
puts on his backpack and goes to the cemetery's
park.

55. EXT. CEMETERY PARK - DAY

Mike walks through the quiet streets, the wind
stirring the leaves of the nearby trees. APRIL
finds relief among the graves in the cemetery park.
Mike sees APRIL and runs over.

                         MIKE
                       (Loudly)
             APRIL! APRIL! I am coming.

APRIL doesn't turn around but still stares at one
place, as if talking to it. Mike hurries over and
holds APRIL in his arms.

                         MIKE
             APRIL, I'm here. You have been wronged.

                        APRIL
             I seek relief among the graves.

                         MIKE

I'll pay your rent.

APRIL's shock and realization mix on her face.

APRIL

Thank you but I do not like this. I don't know whether my dad is dead or alive. I don't know where my mother lives after being kicked out. I was so helpless and penniless. I don't want to go back.

MIKE

I can help you.

APRIL

You helped me today, but you can't help me tomorrow. I think of the homeless guy 404.

APRIL cries so sadly.

MIKE

APRIL, you remember I said I have a way to make money. Baby, why did you forget it? Why don't you give me some pressure? Don't worry too much.

APRIL

I understand that you may not be able
to help me. If you want to do it, you
could have done it long ago. I am also
looking for other jobs. I have to rely
on myself.

MIKE

Marry me and I will be responsible for
you.

APRIL

No, this is impossible; this is too out
of love is love. Reality is reality.
Tears are the comfort when a woman is
in despair.

MIKE

Although I know that you are telling
the truth and tearing the veil of love.
But I...I... When I promised, I didn't
lie to you at that time. I loved you
at that time. However, I never thought
about it at that time.

APRIL

I'm not blaming you.

MIKE

I promised you to go to the casino to gamble and win. You asked me if I have a secret power.

APRIL

But I have never considered the secret power you mentioned real. Is there such an easy pie in the world?

MIKE

Dear, yes. I feel for you now. The camaraderie is real. Now I still promise to pay for your rental fees. Let's go.

APRIL

I will pay you back then.

APRIL stands up with her backpack and is unsteady on her feet. Mike steps up and supports her.

56. INT. YOUTH HOSTEL MIXED GENDER ROOM - DAY

APRIL returns to the youth hostel accompanied by

Mike.

APRIL

Mike, I almost walked into the grave.

MIKE

I have mystical skills. Don't worry
now.

MENG NING leans against the door, looks at APRIL.

MENG NING

Mike didn't humbly accept my inquiries
in pursuit of the truth.

APRIL

Um.

MENG NING

He doesn't look like a rich man.

APRIL

Neither do I.

MENG NING

You look beautiful; you have to respect
yourself.

APRIL looks elsewhere.

MENG NING(CONTINUE)

You are pretending to be crazy again.

APRIL

You see how happy I still am.

MENG NING

I am troubled; I cannot face the debt
I have borne with. Just relax like
watching a play.

APRIL

Aren't you debt-free?

MENG NING

That's you; your uncle lost the house
and half the restaurant. What else do
I have? What else do you have? I just
want to bet more and have fun.

APRIL

You said you swore not to gamble? Did
you do it again?

MENG NING

Nonsense, don't you want to go too?
It's so cruel. Every time I go, I feel
like I've fallen into some kind of
trap. Your kind-hearted aunt XU MEILI
knew it.

APRIL

What's happened to her?

MENG NING

Nothing, she's fine. That's like
a madhouse restaurant. It's a
crematorium. Don't go.

APRIL

Money, and - when it goes useless.

MENG NING

APRIL, money is useful at any time. It
is absolutely true. Indeed, especially
for women.

APRIL

Really?

MENG NING

You have no money, and you want to
be a poet. You are daydreaming!Don't

even hope that you can be. Especially
women. The first day I got here, all
my money was stolen. There's no point
calling the police. They don't
care. You should leave the place
quickly.

MENG NING goes back to her room after she finishes
her conversation. She quickly packs her things,
and leaves without even saying farewell to APRIL.

57.INT. TANG RESTAURANT - DAY

LI JIANSHE is sighing.

> **LI JIANSHE**
> Really. Close the door and let us drink
> the northwest wind.

> **MENG NING**
> It's too cold to have no money.

> **LI JIANSHE**
> You ran away and you dared to come
> back.

> **MENG NING**

You know what I saw was surprising?
APRIL fooled around with a poor guy.

LI JIANSHE

She looks like an angel to me, even if
she sleeps on the street, she's still
an angel and better than you.

MENG NING

Are you attracted to her?

At this time, APRIL walks in from the back door
of the restaurant. LI JIANSHE greets.

APRIL

Aunt MEILI is coming over later.

LI JIANSHE quickly calls MENG NING who was hiding
in the Back out.

LI JIANSHE

Go and leave here quickly.

LI JIANSHE follows MENG NING to leave.

XU MEILI comes. She walks directly to APRIL.

> **XU MEILI**
>
> Calculate the turnover and apply for
> government funding.

APRIL then looks for forms on the computer and
paper information on the checkout counter. Slowly,
time passes.

> **APRIL**
>
> Auntie, it's almost done.

> **XU MEILI**
>
> You can do it again tomorrow. You can't
> take the bus too late. You leave. I'll
> take a taxi back later.

APRIL tidies up.

> **APRIL**
>
> Okay, I'll go first.

58.INT.TANG RESTAURANT - NIGHT

Outside the door, MENG NING quietly returns to
the restaurant. Seeing the lights on inside, she
quietly peeks in from the door cracks and Finds
XU MEILI lying on the ground. She walks over. XU

MEILI's eyes are closed, she is confused, and her mouth is crooked.

MENG NING

Hi.

MENG NING turns to pick up XU MEILI's arm and puts it down again. She picks up her phone and dials 911.

MENG NING

Someone here needs emergency help.

While waiting for the ambulance, MENG NING looks at the scene in the restaurant with worry.

59. INT. EMERGENCY ROOM - DAY

XU MEILI wakes up slowly, opens her eyes, and feels dizzy. MENG NING stands beside her bed, watching her with concern. XU MEILI tried to say a few words, but her voice was a little hoarse.

XU MEILI

I... had a stroke.

MENG NING

I found you. I called 911 right away,

and otherwise, you are in danger.

XU MEILI squeezes out a few words between her
lips.

                    XU MEILI

Where is APRIL?

                    MENG NING

She has long since disappeared. Thank
God I arrived in time.

                    XU MEILI

Thanks.

60.INT.YOUTH HOSTEL - KITCHEN - EVENING

MIKE uses the computer in the public kitchen room.
MENG NING walks in.

                    MENG NING

I am coming again.

                    MIKE

You would like to come at night.

                    MENG NING

Yes, I told you that on the phone.

                    MIKE

Is APRIL in big trouble?

                 MENG NING

Not a big trouble. As long as you are
willing to help me, do you have money?

                    MIKE

No, I am almost bankrupt.

                 MENG NING

That's better that you need money.

                    MIKE

What do you want me to do? Tell me
quickly.

                 MENG NING

Find   a   doctor   who   can   evaluate
euthanasia.

MENG NING walks across the table and sits directly
on Mike's lap. She holds Mike's face and leans
against Mike with her chest. Mike feels hot.

MIKE

What are you going to do?

MENG NING

I want you.

MENG NING's butt falls off Mike's lap. Mike stands up. He is used to not wearing a belt to fasten his belt. His pants fall down. MENG NING pulls on the top of Mike's pants, Pushes Mike towards the room.

61. EXT. MOUNTAIN ROAD - DAY

MIKE drives and parks the car on a higher road, the sea on the right and the hillside on the left. APRIL points to the roots of a tree on the hillside across the road that is knocked down by heavy wind, rain and water.

APRIL

I admire this tree very much.

Mike takes APRIL's arm and then takes APRIL's hand. They walk on the drizzling hillside path toward the old tree that is dead but still has thick roots. They walk towards the roots of the tree. The sun shows its face a little.

MIKE

Hey, where are your magic glasses?

APRIL

Oh, I haven't used it in a few days. They are in
the bag.

MIKE

Don't lose it.

APRIL

Of course, I won't. Otherwise, I would
lose a lot of money.

MIKE

The main thing is that bad people
cannot take it away.

APRIL

Why?

MIKE

Well, I'll tell you later.

The two of them return to the car. Mike drives.
They pass by a scenic road with the sea on one

side and mountains on the other, and then on the
flat land between mountains and deep curves.

AI ONION (V.O)

The catharsis of the soul, tears
running, requires no composition.
The saddest echoes remain concealed,
no one song required.The rain is
desperate; don't let the sleeping
window hear it.Some inquiring ears
sleeping inside.

APRIL puts her cell phone to her ear.

APRIL

Hi, my beautiful aunt's phone number
can't be reached either.

MIKE

You don't go to her. You just relax
today.

62.INT. YOUTH HOSTEL KITCHEN - EVENING

APRIL cooks a lot of Chinese dishes in the public
kitchen. APRIL wears a red cheongsam. Her slim
waist is made subtle and gentle by the close-

fitting cheongsam. She is skillful. Every movement appears poetic and picturesque. APRIL skillfully cuts vegetables with knives. She handles the fresh ingredients in an orderly manner. The red cheongsam rips under her elegant movements, making her look even more graceful.

                    MIKE
                  (Admire)
        The skirt is very mysterious, and seems
        to be very interesting, and seems to
        be talking.

                   APRIL
        (Smiling, putting down his tools)
        This is a Chinese cheongsam. I only
        wear it during the holidays to express
        my happiness. Today you have to eat
        rice.

Each of the five dishes emits dazzling color and aroma, filling the table. Mike can't help but watch all this with excitement. Mike goes over to hug APRIL and kisses her cheek. APRIL smiles brightly, turning her face a little shy. Mike leans close to APRIL's ear.

                        MIKE

Thanks for the happiest birthday. I'm
really happy to have you.

Just as they are getting together, Mike's cell
phone rings. He answers the call.

                        MIKE
                (Take a deep breath)
It was Luo Qian who called. She said
she was in trouble now.

                        APRIL

Luo Qian came to me and asked me if I
needed money, and she lent me $20,000.

                        MIKE

I also need money recently to make
more money. I borrowed some loans, if
I can't pay back the money, they will
kill me.

                        APRIL

Ah... Ah... Would you like me to
urgently assist you with this $20,000?

MIKE falling into thought, finally nodded.

> **MIKE**
>
> Really? That's so kind of you; I'll
> pay the interest to Luo Qian.

63. INT.YOUTH HOSTEL - MIXED-GENDER ROOM - NIGHT

MIKE and APRIL lie separately on their beds. MIKE
stand up and lie next to APRIL.

> **MIKE**
>
> Valentine's Day is tonight, my baby.

MIKE hugs APRIL on her bed. APRIL is a little
pushy him away, but MIKE seals APRIL's mouth with
his mouth.

> **APRIL**
>
> Don't.

MIKE hugs her forcefully, pressing his whole body
on his body. She struggles to escape but obeys.

64. INT. YOUTH HOSTEL MIXED GENDER ROOM - NEXT MORNING

APRIL cries on her bed. MIKE is still sleeping.
MIKE's cell phone rings. He turns it off in a daze.

APRIL

I'm really sad.

MIKE

Don't feel bad; it was fun. Real
couples can't compare with us.

MIKE picks up his phone and looks at the time.

MIKE

I'm going to be late. I need to get
out right away.

65. INT. JACK'S OFFICE - DAY

Boss Jack is in a meeting with ELLIE and Mike.

JACK

The AI robots ONION and JASMINE are
at odds with each other.Yes, the
onion is replicating itself after
getting angry.

MIKE

AI ONION's mood was messed up, and so
was AI JASMINE's. An error has occurred
in the programmed main control AI.

JACK

It appears that the AI and the test's
owner may have developed a connection
of feelings. This is what we had hoped
for.

ELLIE

The script is dangerous. Robots will
have emotions like humans. Are you
feeling emotional?

JACK

Remember, we have taken a great step.
Remember, we cannot develop feelings
for the person being tested; otherwise,
we will lose all investments.

MIKE

I'm transforming these robots.

66.INT. CASINO - NIGHT

Mike finally finds a woman in her forties, wearing
black clothes and light black lipstick.

MIKE

Luo Qian, the money I lent you has
been overdue for a long time.You must
pay me back today.

LUO QIAN

They transferred all the money in the
casino to China. I am also a victim.

MIKE grabs the clothes on LUO QIAN's chest and
becomes furious.

MIKE

Do you want me to die? You should die
first!

LUO QIAN

Your parents left you enough money to
spend your whole life.

MIKE

Asshole! Swindler! I lost everything
and took out loan sharks.

LUO QIAN

You asked me to find your friend APRIL
and lend her the money.I can't pay it
back. I'm in debt.

MIKE

You devil, she gave me her money too.

LUO QIAN

Your mysterious gambling power is not
working. You are the only one. It's
the devil.

MIKE

(Push Luo Qian to the wall)
What kind of power I have is none of
your business. Don't talk nonsense.

67. INT. HOSPITAL - ROM - DAY

XU MEILI still slowly learning to say a few words.

MENG NING

You have been sick for so long. APRIL
never showed up. Thank God now she can
finally visit you.

APRIL walks in. As soon as APRIL sees XU MEILI,
she quickly walks over and hugs XU MEILI's head
and cries.

APRIL

Sorry, I just found out.

XU MEILI

MENG NING saved me. Why did you leave
first that day?

APRIL

Sorry, you asked me to leave first.

XU MEILI

(Thinking deeply)

Um.

68. INT. NIGHTCLUB - NIGHT

MIKE and APRIL find a seat at the nightclub. APRIL
takes off her coat and puts it next to her. The two
of them order drinks and start drinking.

MIKE

I was broke and had my money stolen.
The company you are testing your AI
with is my employer. I have nothing
now.

APRIL

What?

MIKE

The master AI I programmed made an error. I can't win money from gambling anymore. The magic of the AI is broken.

APRIL was sick. She gets up and goes to the toilet. Mike picks up APRIL's coat. He takes out the wallet inside, Mike, takes out two hundred dollars given by Sophie's daughter. He takes $100 cash and pays for the drinks. A DRUNK MAN detects Mike's stealing in the dark. When he finds Mike walking away, he immediately approaches and takes APRIL's coat away. APRIL comes back and continues drinking, getting very high.

MIKE

Sorry, I have to leave first. Let's go Dutch. I've already paid.

APRIL drunkenly looks at Mike and smiles.

APRIL

You are such a liar.

MIKE leaves.

APRIL looks around anxiously for her coat. Then the drunken man staggers over and hands her a card. She looks at him and sees that it is her driver's license.

DRUNKEN MAN

You look so pitiful.

APRIL

(Crying and frightened)
Someone took my wallet, my clothes.

DRUNKEN MAN

Ha-ha, they are in my car.

69. EXT. CITY STREET - MIDNIGHT

A car stops on the side of the road. The two men drag another person out of the car. They dump the person in a hidden place on the street and then drive away. The sky slowly grows brighter. The red light of the sunrise illuminates the girl's face. She opens her eyes; her body aches, and she looks around, wondering what has been going on.

(Flashback)

The scene of the seaside cemetery being flooded and then resurfaced, MIKE pointing there.

APRIL

How ashamed I am, how happy I am under the light of the streetlamp. Cry in coldness.

AI ONION (V.O)

The approaching sounds are vague, like robbers or rapists.

AI JASMINE (V.O)

Momentary fear clamouring in the mind is not death.

APRIL

I'm alive.

AI ONION (V.O)

The rain is beating on it.

APRIL

Are you here to terrorize me?

AI JASMINE (V.O)

They are like a mighty army with

thousands of horses.

                            APRIL

I only have one life, not enough for
you to stretch out your fingers.

Suddenly, a hand pulls APRIL's foot. APRIL looks
back in horror and sees that it is HOMELESS 404.
The HOMELESS man recognizes her. He pulls a piece
of clothing from his cart, which is filled with
rags.

                            APRIL

You, 404?

                        HOMELESS 404

Yes, are you cold?

APRIL is shivering all over her body. She nods and
the man puts the clothes on her.

70. EXT. CITY STREET - EARLY MORNING

The early risers see her, and find she is still
alive. She stands up unsteadily. There is a large
lake nearby, and she can see the water.

71. EXT. LAKESIDE - DAY

APRIL approaches the lake step by step. She steps in the shallow water, and the HOMELESS man pushes his cart, looking left and right, smiling and following APRIL.

The wind picks up, like a rotating wind, blowing up the clothes, blankets and other messy, smelly things in the HOMELESS's car. He chases them in the wind. The rain starts to fall again. APRIL walks slowly into the water.

> **HOMELESS 404**
> Hey, go down, and go down again, no.
> You stepped in the wrong place.

> **APRIL**
> I don't.

> **HOMELESS 404**
> Don't take away my clothes. There is
> no way down there.

> **APRIL**
> What clothes?

> ### HOMELESS 404
>
> Wear it on you.

> ### APRIL
>
> I'm going to die.

> ### HOMELESS 404
>
> My clothes can't die.

> ### APRIL
>
> Isn't my life worth less than your
> clothes?

HOMELESS 404 points to the wet properties in his shopping cart.

> ### HOMELESS 404
>
> I don't want to die yet. I still have
> so many clothes.

APRIL turns his head and looks at the HOMELESS blankly. It is as if the HOMELESS's words saved her. She walks out of the shallow water silently. The rain is dripping on her.

> ### APRIL
>
> Why are you 404?

HOMELESS 404

404 is a code. I have a PhD in Computer
science. Later I lost my job. I became
poor and lost my family. I still have
psychopathic depression.

APRIL

I'll take you to eat dumplings.

HOMELESS 404

(Smile)

Good. Thank you! It's good to be alive.
I hid my cart first.

72. INT. XU MEILI'S HOME - DAY

XU MEILI slowly recovers in bed. Her original fat
body looks a little swollen. The nanny is busy
taking care of her. MENG NING walks in, takes out
a piece of paper and shows it to her. She also
puts a piece of newspaper on the bed. A piece of
news on euthanasia shows. XU MEILI looked at the
data on the paper.

XU MEILI

Well, the expenses are quite high.

XU MEILI picks up the newspaper, glancing at it.

XU MEILI

Now I can only lie down, sit in a wheelchair, and feel lonely. It's better to leave this world. The regulations of euthanasia fit me.

MENG NING

You must not think like this.

XU MEILI

I need all-around care. I might as well burn myself first before the money is used up. Don't you also want me to die?

MENG NING is beside the bed with a sad expression.

MENG NING

You'll be fine if you get to the hospital earlier that day.

XU MEILI

You are wrong. I asked APRIL to leave first on the day I became ill.

MENG NING

Okay?

XU MEILI

If I sell my house, will I pay off the
mortgage? You can give it to APRIL,
and you can also pay her father
FULAI's bail. I have already written
a will.

MENG NING

Do you want euthanasia to leave money
for APRIL and her father? A gambling
father?

XU MEILI

I owe it. I owe wages to APRIL's
mother. They helped me when I needed
it most. I feel sorry for them.

MENG NING

You forgot; you already asked me to
give that gambling father bail first.

73. INT. TANG RESTAURANT - DAY

The restaurant is closed. LI JIANSHE and MENG NING are talking at the door of the kitchen.

MENG NING

This is why euthanasia is necessary.

LI JIANSHE

What? Yellow-faced woman, she wants to end her life that way? APRIL will persuade her to change her mind.

MENG NING

Now it was my turn to despair. She wants the remaining money to go to APRIL and her parents. She is crazy. Don't tell APRIL.

74. INT. XU MEILI'S HOME - DAY

Mike takes out the doctor's report on XU MEILI's euthanasia.

MENG NING

The will also states that the property belongs to APRIL. Is this your true wish?

XU MEILI

Yes. Don't you have a share?

                    MENG NING

I know your wish. I don't want the
dispute to affect your euthanasia
decision.

                    XU MEILI

Yes, can you be more peaceful?

                    MENG NING

It will, I promise. I'll be the executor
of the will.

                    XU MEILI

Um.

                    MENG NING

 Yes, you can put it down in your will.

                    XU MEILI

You can't change me anymore.

75.EXT. ON THE BUS - DAY

APRIL sits on a bus facing the door. Her bag,
glasses and cell phone are placed on the right

seat. A large transparent plastic bag on the ground is full of bottles and cans for recycling. She suddenly speaks to herself in a casual and self-righteous manner. HOMELESS 404 sits to her left.

                         APRIL

     It's snowing, hurry up to sweep the
     snow. That house is falling.

Some passengers look outside of the window, where the sun is shining brightly, and then look at her. Everybody is quiet.

                         APRIL

     Look, it's raining.

APRIL seems to have no one in her eye. When the bus arrives at a stop, she gets off. HOMELESS 404 follows closely behind. The two entered the restaurant.

76.I/E.TANG RESTAURANT - DAY

APRIL enters the restaurant. TANG JIN recognizes APRIL. He is shocked and speechless. Tang Jin quickly goes to the cabinet and gets a pack of medicine.

TANG JIN

This is the medicine your mother asked
someone to send to you. She said it
was poisonous and should be properly
stored.

APRIL

Yes, it is used to treat depression.

She takes in the medicine with water. APRIL opens
the refrigerator and takes out a pack of dumplings.

APRIL

(To HOMELESS 404)
Can I cook you some dumplings?

The sound of fire trucks comes from far and near.
APRIL is awakened. She quickly walks to the window
to look outside. TANG JIN also runs over to see
what happened. They see a fire truck roaring towards
them.

APRIL

Hey, why did you stop?

Two people get out of the fire truck and go

straight to the restaurant. They first look at
the firefighting facilities near the door.

FIREFIGHTER

We routinely inspect this house for
safety.

Not long after, the firefighters leave.

TANG JIN

Your beautiful aunt is going to be
euthanized today.

APRIL

Ah, how is that possible, I don't know!
We now go talk to her out of it!

TANG JIN

Nothing we can do now. Can you go to
say goodbye?

APRIL

We have to rescue her and make her
change her mind.

TANG JIN

It's too late. MENG NING blocked

things.

Firefighters return.

                    FIREFIGHTER
     This restaurant needs to be closed for
     safety issues.

77.I/E. XU MEILI'HOME - DAY

XU MEILI lies on the bed and hugs everyone one by
one. Everyone lines up to say goodbye to her.

                    XU MEILI
          (Whispering in APRIL's ear)
     APRIL, I promised you real estate
     before. I have no children. I treat
     you as my daughter. But the legal
     executor is MENG NING. After paying
     the fee to MENG NING, there should be
     enough money to pay the wages owed to
     you and your mother.

                    APRIL
     Auntie, money is not important, what
     is important is you can SURVIVE.
     I beg you to change your mind.

MENG NING comes over.

> **MENG NING**
>
> People behind are lining up to say
> goodbye.

She pulls APRIL aside.

> **MENG NING**
>
> I heard that you are sick. Go to the
> casino to try your luck. I'm going
> tonight to get rid of the bad luck.

> **APRIL**
>
> I don't want to go.

> **MENG NING**
>
> I have some money for you, and you
> will know when you get there.

APRIL comes out and cries softly.

> **APRIL**
>
> (To herself)
>
> This is not death, she is still alive,
> but tears and snot suffocate me.

APRIL sees her mother. She runs over and throws herself at her mother.

APRIL

Mom, can we not let my aunt die? I'm sorry. I shouldn't be angry with you. It is my fault. Please forgive me.

JIA SHUYA

APRIL it's my fault. You forgive me.

MENG NING

(To APRIL)

She chose three minutes of euthanasia.

MENG NING asks everyone to go outside. KONG FULAI arrives out of expectation. He walks directly into the room with a painful look on his face. When the doctor arrives, Tang Jin greets him, and they walk into the room together with KONG FULAI. Soon, Tang Jin and KONG FULAI came out. APRIL throws herself on her father and cries bitterly. Her mother also comes over. The three of them hugged each other.

KONG FULAI

Dad loves you. Let's pray together
for Auntie Mei for her to go to heaven.

                    APRIL
                 (Crying)
I will never see my aunt again.

[Flashback]

78. EXT. CITY STREET - DAY

APRIL, AI Onion and AI JASMINE are all lying on
the street. HOMELESS man 404 next to them stands
watching.

                    APRIL
               (Looking at the sky)
The pain is so lonely, there are only
tears.

               AI ONION
Everyone is asleep.

               AI JASMINE
Creepy rain.

               AI ONION

Active fear among the trees.

79.INT.TANG RESTAURANT - DAY

Tang Jin, LI JIANSHE and APRIL sit at the table in a daze. The fire rectification notice is placed on the table.

                    LI JIANSHE
    Are you saying that this house cannot
    be lived in?

                    TANG JIN
    It costs a lot of money to fix the
    problems. No business is allowed now.

                    APRIL
    So where can we go?

                    TANG JIN
    This building is a cultural relic
    protection project designated by the
    government, as this is a crematorium
    history that cannot be rebuilt.

                    LI JIANSHE
    The boss lady has gone to heaven. Are

we going to hell?

80. I/E TOUR BUS SQUARE - NIGHT

Five or six people are lining up in the office to register. A large tour bus on the square is waiting for the gamblers. MENG NING waits. APRIL slowly approaches and timidly looks into the door of the travel agency. She goes in and begins to fill out a form. MENG NING pulls APRIL out and takes out an envelope from her bag.

MENG NING

This is the money XU MEILI left for
you.

Not many people are in the car. APRIL finds a seat and sits down. She takes out a five-dollar free bet and a Buffy meal coupon. She takes out the money from the envelope, a total of five hundred, and then takes out the money from her pocket and puts it on her lap to count. Thirteen pieces of one dollar. She pulls out five from a pile of one dollar bills and counts them again, making a total of eight bills. MENG NING is waiting for someone outside the car.

[Visual angle]

The sky outside is still shrouded in darkness. A little further away, on the other side of the square, the lights of signs and billboards are flashing. She looks closer and sees a familiar figure. It's LI JIANSHE. He gets on the bus, looking for his seat. He is surprised to see APRIL behind him.

> **LI JIANSHE**
> APRIL, it's great to have money. Does everybody want to be rich? I do! There is no need to hide around like a mouse to earn more than a thousand a month.

APRIL turns her head away and continues to look out the window.

81. INT. ON THE BUS - NIGHT LATER

A fashionable woman wears a close-fitting silk shirt with two open collars and a beautiful silk scarf tied around her neck. It's MENG NING. She gets on the bus and attracts the attention of all the gamblers. LI JIANSHE opens his eyes and looks at MENG NING lustfully. She comes over and sits next to LI JIANSHE. APRIL smells a pleasant smell, and so does LI JIANSHE who involuntarily takes a deep breath and wants to throw himself closer to MENG NING. APRIL is surprising, and Mike comes up. APRIL pulls up her mask, not wanting Mike to see her. Mike sits directly next to MENG NING who takes out the cosmetic box from her designer bag and applies eyeliner vigorously in front of the small mirror. After a while, the bus was full. APRIL notices all the people's eyes are full of the light of getting rich. The bus starts, and slowly drives out of the square, out of the city, and into the darkness. Everyone on the bus closes their eyes, and APRIL is alone looking out the window with her eyes open...

82. EXT. OUTSIDE THE CASINO - NIGHT

This casino is not as luxurious as the legendary casino in Las Vegas. It is a separate building. The parking lot outside the gate is very large. People get off one by one. APRIL put on the AI glasses, and she knows that she can't avoid Mike.

83. INT. INSIDE THE AI GLASSES - NIGHT

APRIL enters the glasses and looks at the two AIs in silence.

AI JASMINE

You have to be careful today. ONION said he wanted to fight me.

AI ONION

There must be a scary person inside.

AI JASMINE

I never thought it would save me.

APRIL

From here, I would run away; the cement road was full of potholes.

[Flashback]

84. INT. JACK'S OFFICE - DAY

JAKE

AI ONION has escaped us and has been entering the self-reproduction stage.

ELLIE

It seems to have symptoms of mental retardation or depression, and it is a feeling.

JACK

No, it probably has self-editing
capabilities and is just messed up.

ELLIE

What to do about AI JASMINE, should we
stop testing?

JACK

It may be too late, they are wild and
indulgent, not subject to our control.

85. INT. CASINO - DAY

APRIL walks slowly, not knowing where to go. After
entering the door, LI JIANSHE walks a few steps
back and comes to APRIL's side. APRIL is puzzled,
wondering why he is so listless.

LI JIANSHE

What do you play first?

APRIL shakes her head, expressing his casualness.

APRIL

The kind that wins big money.

LI JIANSHE laughs and looks at APRIL's ignorance
and greed with pity.

LI JIANSHE

Are you crazy about getting rich? Play
big and lose miserably, play tiger
Machine. How much?

APRIL

Five hundred or more.

LI JIANSHE laughs again.

APRIL remains silent and follows LI JIANSHE
through the door to the counter where chips are
exchanged. They come to the slot machine. LI
JIANSHE and APRIL first stuff a coin into the money
slot, starting to play. Soon the coin is swallowed
by the slot machine.

LI JIANSHE

Your glasses are very mysterious. Will
they help you win?

LI JIANSHE leaves for the restroom. APRIL starts
playing herself. She is lucky at first, but after

playing for a while, the coin seems to have fallen
into a deep well. The sweet dinging sound of the
slot machine turns into the terrifying sound of
coin eating. She looks at the coins on the table.
Only a few coins left. A hundred-dollar coins
are almost gone. Sweat begins to perspire on her
forehead. Pop the last few into the tiger's mouth.
Then she loses all. APRIL holds her head in her
hands. All she gets in response is a ding-dong-
ding-dong sound as a compliment to her coins.
There are only a few coins left; she panics and
takes a deep breath in her mouth every time she
inserts a coin. But the slot machine keeps eating
the coins in her eyes. It's all about gambling
again.

86. INT. CASINO - NIGHT

She sits in front of the slot machine, clasps
her hands together, and murmurs: Bless me please.
Bless me please. She starts stuffing silver coins
into the slot. APRIL put the last coins into the
slot but the last batch of coins makes no difference
and is swallowed again. She gets up and walks
outside. Passing by the blackjack table, she sees
Tang Jin and LI JIANSHE sitting there with chips
piled in front of them, smiling happily.

87.EXT. CASINO - EARLY MORNING

Outside the casino, looking at the stars in the sky, APRIL takes a deep breath and looks at her phone.

[Close-up]

It is four o'clock in the morning. APRIL sits on a stone step. She touches her pocket; there isn't a penny in it. Instead, an uncomfortable smell of smoke comes from behind. She hears Mike's voice followed by MENG NING's voice. She quickly walks aside so that she can avoid them.

> MENG NING
>
> You lose miserably. Have a cigarette?

> MIKE
>
> You know who I am now; I'm a pauper now. Yes, if you have money, lend me some and I can offer you high interest.

> MENG NING
>
> You don't have to ask me to borrow money, you just need to help me, and

the money will come to you.

MIKE

Is it tonight?

MIKE takes out a cigarette from MENG NING's cigarette case, lights it up and slowly blows out the smoke.

A gust of cool wind blew, and April shivers.

[Cut]

APRIL sits there quietly alone. She puts a leaf in her mouth, raises her lips together, blows gently, and gently turns the leaf with her fingers.

[Close up]

Her father's face looms in the smoke, and he says to JIA SHUYA: The loan shark demands repayment of 20,000 dollars, dollars, dollars...

Suddenly a voice comes from behind.

LI JIANSHE

APRIL, are you waiting for the bus

outside? You have to wait three or
four hours for the bus. Let's go and
play inside!

APRIL shakes her head, but LI JIANSHE has no
intention of giving up.

APRIL

I don't want to gamble anymore. I will
only lose.

LI JIANSHE takes out a stack of hundred-dollar
banknotes from his pocket and hands dozens of
them to APRIL.

LI JIANSHE

APRIL, take this one thousand.

APRIL is frightened and resists.

LI JIANSHE

Now you are here, otherwise, I will
lose everything.

Before APRIL can react, LI JIANSHE stuffs the money
into APRIL's hand, and returns to the casino.
APRIL chases after him.

88. INT. CASINO - LATER NIGHT

The waitress comes over. MENG NING takes two glasses of Whiskey,sits down at an empty table, and toasts to Mike.

MENG NING

May all your wishes come true!

Mike's vision is blurred. MENG NING in front of him turns into APRIL. Mike grabs her hand.

MIKE

Don't leave me.

89. INT. CASINO - POKER ROOM - EARLY MORNING I

LI JIANSHE

(Shouts)

It's once-in-a-lifetime luck. Here comes a big one today.

90. INT. CASINO - RESTAURANT - LATER NIGHT

APRIL and MENG NING sit face to face in the box

seats. APRIL's backpack is placed between the seats with MENG NING.

                    MENG NING

Your glasses are worth a lot of money.

                     APRIL

Maybe.

                    MENG NING

Do you know Tang Jin promises me everything?

                     APRIL

Liar! You are the mistress yourself! No, It's a tragedy. Can you bear the overwhelming abuse?

                    MENG NING

I can't control that much anymore. If you rely solely on hard work for decades, you will still end up poor.

APRIL looked to the side.

                     APRIL

I don't want to give up on myself.

MENG NING

Are you scolding me for giving up on
myself? Then what do you want, give me
your Mike? Give me happiness!

APRIL puts her face in her hands in pain. MENG
NING secretly picks up APRIL's bag, touches the
AI glasses, takes them out, puts them in her bag,
stands up, and leaves some tips.

91. INT. CASINO - CHIP COUNTER - LATER NIGHT

LI JIANSHE lines up in front of the chip counter,
holding a basket full of chips in his hand. He
calculates that it was a full fifty or sixty
thousand dollars. He is humming a tune that no
one has heard before. LI JIANSHE turns around and
sees APRIL holding one thousand dollars in cash.
He pulls APRIL to a hiding place.

APRIL

It's your money.

LI JIANSHE looks at APRIL with fascination, then
walks over and pinches APRIL's breasts with his
hand.

LI JIANSHE

I won big. The money is all yours.

APRIL looks a little dazed and looks at LI JIANSHE
with disdain.

LI JIANSHE

You are beautiful, much better than
MENG NING.

LI JIANSHE's bare head, with only a few hairs
left, glows brightly.

LI JIANSHE

Marry me.

As LI JIANSHE speaks, he leans against APRIL, hugs
APRIL, kisses APRIL'S FACE, and grabs APRIL's
breasts with his hands.

APRIL breaks away from him. She throws all the
money in her hand at LI JIANSHE's face, and then
walks towards a crowded place.

92.I/E. CASINO - LATER NIGHT

TANG JIN loses so much that he doesn't know what

to do. He drinks a lot. The waitress comes over
with wine. MENG NING happens to come to find him.
TANG JIN is startled and takes a step back. MENG
NING takes Tang Jin's arm and walks towards the
door. APRIL follows quietly.

> **MENG NING**
>
> Come on, go outside and get some fresh
> air. Will calm your mind.

> **TANG JIN**
>
> Didn't I already give you money? Are
> you going to force me?

> **MENG NING**
>
> You agreed to divorce Yellow Faced
> woman, and you hung on for so long.
> That day, if I hadn't left early, I
> would have been in the funeral home.

> **TANG JIN**
>
> They forced me and all the property
> was lost. The hotel is only half
> left.

MENG NING's full head of hair leans against TANG
JIN.

> **MENG NING**
> The salted fish cannot turn over. There
> is only a dead end.

MENG NING looks back at APRIL.

> **MENG NING**
> Where are your energy glasses? Why
> don't you wear it? It will lose its
> magic power. Come on.

APRIL IGNORES MENG NING, AND APPROACHES TANG JIN.

> **APRIL**
> Uncle, let's get out of here.

APRIL picks up his bag and finds that her AI
glasses are missing. He is horrified and looks
everywhere for them.

93. INT. CASINO CHIP COUNTER - LATER NIGHT

After cashing the chips, LI JIANSHE takes a check
for $100,000 dollars and more than $5,000 in cash.
When he comes out, the waitress walks by with a
wine tray. LI JIANSHE takes a glass of red wine
to calm down his excitement. APRIL looks for her
glasses. She stands nearby, watching silently and

helplessly. Tang Jin comes over behind APRIL, holding a hundred dollars in his hand.

                    TANG JIN
                 (To LI JIANSHE)
          The beauty is not shallow.

                    MENG NING
          A dead fish, lose your bottom pants.

                    TANG JIN
                 (To LI JIANSHE)
          Everything is lost. Can you lend me
          some?

LI JIANSHE feels a little unbearable when he sees tang Jin almost begging. MENG NING leaves subconsciously.

                    LI JIANSHE
          TANG JIN! Let's have a cigarette
          outside.

TANG JIN follows LI JIANSHE out and waits for Li JIANSHE to answer his question.

94. EXT. CASINO - STAIRS - EARLY MORNING

It's extremely dark before dawn. LI JIANSHE takes a puff of cigarette and blows out the smoke rings deeply. Tang Jin doesn't dare to look at him.

LI JIANSHE

In addition to restaurants, you also have stocks, trading company shares, luxury homes worth millions. The car you drive is a Rolls Royce. How come you have no money to gamble?

TANG JIN

The gamble is over. I am penniless, and in a desperate situation with no solution.

[cut]

Mike comes out from behind MENG NING. APRIL looks up at MENG NING with a strange look.

MIKE

Hey APRIL.

APRIL looks at Mike and nods. MENG NING takes out a pack of cigarettes from her bag. She then lights up the cigarette skillfully and holds the cigarette between her fingers. Tang Jin also comes over.

MENG NING

(To APRIL)

You don't seem to have any energy at all.

APRIL

(Crying)

My AI glasses are missing; can you help me find them? I stopped gambling; the slot machines took all my money.

MENG NING

(To Mike)

You said that AI glasses are very valuable. If someone offers a high price, go find them quickly.

MIKE

What do you mean? What glasses? I have lost miserably myself.

TANG JIN

I also lost everything.

MENG NING

(To Tang Jin)

You look so wilted; you have no future.

When TANG JIN hears MENG NING say this. His pride is hurt.

MIKE

People cannot afford to lose! Life is just a gamble. You'll die if you take the gamble.

MENG NING

(To TANG JIN)

Don't dare. Yes, why are you coming to the United States?

TANG JIN's heart is completely injured.

TANG JIN

Get a job, open a shop, earn some money, and pay off my debts, already I am so lucky.

TANG JIN'S heart is burning, and he is about to have an attack. MENG NING leaves.

MIKE

Boss TANG, you will win it back today, and so will I. Let's get some more chips.

TANG JIN

Now the only option is to find LI JIANSHE.

MIKE

LI JIANSHE is counting his money, so let's go and look.

95. INT. BESIDE GAMBLING TABLE — EARLY MORNING

MIKE and MENG NING walk over with drinks when APRIL stops MIKE.

APRIL

MIKE, I have something to tell you.

MIKE asks MENG NING to leave first, and MENG NING leaves reluctantly.

APRIL

MIKE, you forgot the oath you swore, you said you were good at gambling.

There is magic power for winning money
at the table.

MIKE

I haven't forgotten it! I felt so bad
that MENG NING took the initiative to
come and find me. Besides, my magic
weapon is your glasses, you lost your
AI glasses and I'm not sure.

APRIL

Why didn't you mention what glasses
have to do with you before?

MIKE

Because my boss wants me to keep it
secret. So, I didn't disclose it to
anyone. You see, I am so poor now. You
bought me a bet.

APRIL

And MENG NING!

MIKE

Yes, and she. But I can always try, as
long as you can support me.

APRIL suddenly remembers that MENG NING mentioned
that she has glasses several times.

                    APRIL
    Mike, wait by the table while I look
    for the glasses.

96. INT. CASINO – EARLY MORNING

APRIL sees MENG NING sitting in a bar drinking,
with several foreign men next to her, laughing.
MENG NING looks a little drunk. APRIL is about
to ask MENG NING if she steals the AI glasses.
MENG NING glances at her in confusion, covers her
mouth and runs to the bathroom.

APRIL grabs MENG NING's handbag, opens it and sees
that the pair of glasses is in her bag. APRIL puts
on her glasses, and two AIs immediately appear in
front of her.

                  AI JASMINE
    Where have you been? Why did you abandon
    us, this woman Almost destroyed us.

                   AI ONION
    Have you met MIKE? Why did he leave

on his own? Are you alone? He is an
ungrateful man.

APRIL

ONION, why do you say that about MIKE?
He is not a bad person; he promised
me that he would win some money from
gambling. Do you know how much money
I need?

97. EXT. CASINO - BY BUSHES - EARLY IN THE MORNING

It's still dark. TANG JIN wipes the corners of his
eyes with his hands. LI JIANSHE's heart trembles
for a while.

TANG JIN

MENG NING asked me to send 500,000
dollars home, and I agreed to her
request. Now even if we sell the car
and restaurant, WE won't get this much
money. I wouldn't come to the casino
if I could help it.

LI JIANSHE

MENG NING is greedy for money, and you

are greedy for sex. What a perfect
match.

APRIL hears this.

TANG JIN

(To APRIL)

Has your beautiful aunt paid you back
the wages she owes you?

APRIL

MENG NING only gave me 500 dollars,
but Aunt MEILI said that she owed my
mother and I more than 100,000 dollars.

TANG JIN

Don't be sad, I'll win it back for
you!

LI JIANSHE

Come to the casino to pay off your
debt. If you gamble for a long time,
you will lose. This is a casino rule.
Not to mention if you are not lucky,
you should find another way to make
money.

TANG JIN

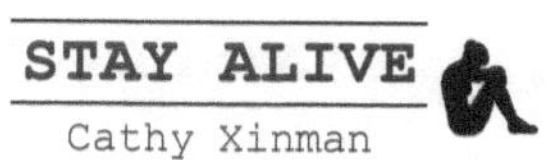

I can't think of any other way.

LI JIANSHE

How much do you want to get a loan
from me?

TANG JIN

Half a million.

LI JIANSHE

Wow, where can I find half a million?

TANG JIN

It is my fault that I shall die.
I will do my best! If you lend me
$50,000, I will give you half of the
equity in the restaurant to you!

APRIL

Uncle TANG, let's go; let's go quickly.
Leave here.

TANG JIN

I won't come home if I don't win today.

TANG JIN writes the contract for LI JIANSHE on
the spot. He signs. LI JIANSHE touches TANG JIN's
trouser pocket.

> LI JIANSHE

TANG JIN, you are so damn lucky to
have the seal in your pocket.

> TANG JIN

Hey, it does.

TANG JIN puts his fingerprint on it. He gives LI
the equity of the restaurant. LI JIANSHE puts all
these papers away.
Then he and TANG JIN walk towards the podium
together. Tang Jin gives APRIL 1,000 dollars in
chips.

> TANG JIN

APRIL, take it, these are the wages
owed to you.

APRIL looks at TANG JIN dumbfounded. TANG JIN
takes the $50,000 chips and walks resolutely to
the casino.

98.INT. CASINO – EARLY MORNING

MIKE sits on the side of the casino; puts on
APRIL's glasses, and the electronic game area

appears inside. He begins to program and focuses on monitoring the performance of the AI programs "ONION" and "JASMINE" he designs on the gaming table.

                    MIKE

                  (Excited)
Onion, JASMINE, we have won five games
in a row, it's a really great success!
We can officially enter the casino.

MIKE took off his glasses and put them on for APRIL.

                    MIKE

Quick. Wear it well. My magic money-
winning power works again. They help me
identify higher- probability winning
positions.

MIKE pulls APRIL back to the casino table. APRIL stands beside him wearing glasses, watching the gambling game intently. MIKE's excitement and anticipation fills the air. APRIL still looks nervous. MIKE 's plan is carried out successfully without being noticed, and he wins a lot of chips.

MIKE

(Whispering in APRIL's ear)

We made a lot of money.

APRIL puts away the winning chips.

APRIL

(Looking at the chips)

We've won enough! We should quit.

The dealer also hesitates to deal with the cards and observes them. Other players begin to observe APRIL, and some follow her in placing bets. Suddenly, A casino STAFF MEMBER also notices something unusual.

99. INT. CASINO - EARLY MORNING

The casino Staff member reports it to the SUPERVISOR. He whispers in the supervisor's ear.

The supervisor immediately calls the casino OWNER. The owner calls Mike's boss, Jack.

OWNER

Jack, you need to look at the robot data right now. This guy MIKE wins too much at our casino.

100. INT. JACK'S HOME OFFICE - EARLY MORNING

JACK immediately connects to the casino control room. He stares at the data on the monitoring screen with his eyes wide open. He immediately begins to modify the program. MIKE and APRIL's luck begins to reverse.

101. INT. - CASINO - EVERY EARLY MORNING

MIKE looks through APRIL's glasses. The AI glasses suddenly perform poorly and begin to miss frequently. MIKE's eyes widen, and APRIL is also stunned.

> MIKE
> (Disappointment)
> Impossible, how could this happen?

They start a losing streak and lose most of the chips they won previously.

> MIKE
> (Angry)
> We were fooled. The AI ONION and JASMINE

in your glasses are both changed.

APRIL grabs the remaining chips on the table.

APRIL

Move!

MIKE

No, I have to continue. Win your money
back.

APRIL

Let's get out of here. I don't want
to gamble anymore. We've already won
enough money. I don't want to lose
them.

MENG NING comes over and walks to MIKE. She sees
the winning chips in APRIL's hand.

MENG NING

(Holding Mike's hand)
Come on; give me more points to win. I
am now a rich woman with money. I'll
invest in you.

APRIL takes Mike's arm and motions for him to

leave quickly. Mike ignores MENG NING and wants
to go out with APRIL.

MENG NING

Do you go with poor APRIL?

MIKE doesn't answer, walks straight out, following
APRIL.

102.EXT. CASINO - PARKING LOT - EARLY MORNING

LI JIANSHE walks to the parking lot. Some folks
are already waiting there. Some are frustrated,
some are happy, some are talking about the dangers
at the gambling table and their skills, and some
are crying. APRIL waits for the bus there for a
long time. She is standing behind a tree. Mike
sees LI JIANSHE's high spirits.

LI JIANSHE is still excited. He lights a cigarette
to calm himself down. He offers MIKE a cigarette.
LI JIANSHE sees MENG NING coming from a distance.
MENG NING takes the cigarette from LI JIANSHE's
hand, lights it, and takes a deep inhalation.
She pulls LI JIANSHE away. APRIL glances at them
and silently waits for the bus. MENG NING and
LI JIANSHE walk far away. APRIL sees MENG NING
laughing and pulling LI JIANSHE. The wind carries

the sound of their conversation.

[Cut]

The camera zooms in on MENG NING and LI JIANSHE.

MENG NING

Won, not just half of the restaurant.

LI JIANSHE

And you…

MENG NING giggles. The camera blurs with laughter.

103.I/E ON THE BUS - EARLY MORNING

Everyone gets on the bus one by one. APRIL sits
at the end. LI JIANSHE and MENG NING deliberately
sit farther away from APRIL. There were still a
few empty seats in the back row of the car. MIKE
walks from the front to the back and sits next to
APRIL. MENG NING SPEAKS QUIETLY TO LI JIANSHE.

MENG NING

If TANG JIN doesn't come, he will
definitely want to die in the casino.

APRIL keeps looking towards the casino door. She doesn't know what she wants to see. She is just looking. The bus starts slowly, and APRIL suddenly shouts.

                    APRIL
     There's another one, there's another
     one. Please wait for him.

The Bus stops slowly, waiting for the man who is running out of breath. The man runs slower and slower, bending down and panting after every few steps. The driver still waits patiently for him to arrive. He opens the automatic door and lets this guy come up. APRIL sees that this person is TANG JIN. He is a little drunk. He climbs onto the bus and stumbles toward the back row. APRIL walks to the bus door and supports TANG JIN. MIKE also comes to help. Several passengers held their noses. The bus drives out of the town and onto the highway. People who are gambling all night doze off. MENG NING falls asleep on LI JIANSHE's shoulder, with her hair spread on LI JIANSHE's chest. LI JIANSHE doesn't sleep and keeps stroking MENG NING's hair. Gradually, everyone in the carriage falls asleep. Only APRIL can't sleep.

[Montage]

Father FULAI appears in front of her, talking to her. He promises her mother that he will send a thousand dollars tomorrow. After a while, AI ONION appears, and he goes to foreign countries and other places, maybe also on the way to the casino. After a while, AI JASMINE appears.

AI ONION

We need to find our way home. I want to find APRIL.

AI JASMINE wears a helmet on her head. She wears large pants. She shouts anxiously to the AI ONION who is bending over to look at her.

AI JASMINE (V.O)

(Loudly)

She must be anxious, but she won't die.

AI ONION (V.O)

No, we will get her back.

AI JASMINE (V.O)

No matter how hard it is, we must get

APRIL back.

AI ONION (V.O)

The breakthrough is complete.

AI JASMINE (V.O)

Death is of no use.

AI ONION (V.O)

Its noise is not worthy of fear.

[Montage]

JIA SHUYA keeps washing her hands under the faucet at home. Her hands are red and cracked, and she is still washing her hands. The sound of running water is still on.

[Flashback]

APRIL's voice in a gender-mixed hostel: I just want a room where I can write poems. MIKE opens his eyes. The bus drives forward rhythmically. APRIL gradually loses consciousness.

104.EXT. TRAVEL AGENCY PLAZA - EARLY MORNING

The bus turns a few corners and arrives at the Travel Agency Plaza, then slowly stops. It opens with a loud noise, the driver shouts. Everyone gets out of the bus in an orderly manner. As the gamblers disperse, the driver shouts loudly to the last, a sleeping guest.

DRIVER

Get off the bus, here we are!

No sound, no movement.

DRIVER[CONT'D]

Alas, it is home now!

No sound, no movement. The driver shouts outside.

DRIVER

Hello! Which passenger knows the passenger behind? You all come back!

[CUT]

MIKE and APRIL walk far away, vaguely hear the driver's panic shouting, turning around and going back. LI JIANSHE and MENG NING also hear the sound. They turn their heads, ignore it, and continue walking away.

APRIL looks to see what is going on and runs the fastest. APRIL gets in the bus.

[CUT]

APRIL is in the bus. MIKE also comes up, and sees that the last person lying there is TANG JIN.

> **APRIL**
> (Holding TANG JIN's head)
> UNCLE, what's wrong with you?

> **MIKE**
> What's wrong with you? Having a heart attack. This is sudden death.

> **DRIVER**
> Call the police!

MIKE is dialing the phone to call the police. The driver sees TANG JIN's head moving and making some noise from his mouth.

> **DRIVER**
> He is not dead. He is alive.

TANG JIN opens his eyes drowsily. Fall asleep again. MIKE immediately turns around.

                    DRIVER
          Do you know this person?

                     MIKE
                     (Nod)
          Call the police quickly.

The driver hurriedly called 911.

105.EXT. STREET / SQUARE - MORNING

Morning is getting brighter, and police cars roar in the distance. Following the police car is an emergency vehicle. MIKE and APRIL are still there. The police walk onto the bus. Other passengers watch from outside the boundary line. TANG JIN is covered with a white cloth on the delivery cart and is pushed out by several people wearing white clothes. TANG JIN on the cart is pushed into the ambulance. The policeman exchanges a few words with the driver. APRIL hurriedly asks the police.

                    APRIL

I am his niece. Can I go with you?

POLICE

No, you need to go on your own. You go to the central hospital for information.

106.INT. HOSPITAL - ICU ROOM - DAY

TANG JIN is lying on the hospital bed; his body is covered with tubes. The room has a light disinfectant smell, and the lights cast soft glows. Footsteps are heard at the door. APRIL gently pushes the door open and enters. Behind her are APRIL's mother and father. APRIL is holding a basket in his hand, filled with fruits and some snacks.

APRIL

(Concernedly)

Uncle, my parents are here to see you.

JIA SHUYA

Brother Tang, are you feeling better?

TANG JIN doesn't respond. His face is pale. APRIL's parents can't help being stunned when they see TANG JIN. The atmosphere in the hospital room is heavy. Tang Jin is suffering from both heart attacks. He opens his eyes and smiles at APRIL and her parents.

                    APRIL

    Uncle, relax. The doctor said you are

    out of danger. You cannot be discharged

    from the hospital within days.

                 KONG FULAI

    Brother, you must be good; we all

    found jobs.

107.EXT. TANG RESTAURANT - DAY

APRIL, MIKE and TANG JIN get out of the bus. APRIL helps TANG JIN to get to the restaurant. The snowflakes are like fine feathers dancing in the wind. APRIL sees HOMELESS 404 at a glance. He is pushing a shopping cart in the snow.

                 HOMELESS 404

    It's snowing; it's snowing. The sky is

    falling.

                    APRIL

    I will take you to see a doctor first.

    Let's find a job together.

[Montage]

The sun shines brightly in the snow; APRIL supports TANG JIN, and MIKE and pushes the HOMELESS 404's shopping cart. They walk together on the sunny road by the river where the drum-shaped granite stones are standing. APRIL runs over by the stone and stands there. APRIL is cleaning the stone with her hand. Everybody is watching her. She stands and cleans the inscription with her sleeves. Then, MIKE calls her.

108.INT. THEATER - EVENING ONE YEAR LATER

The stage is brightly lit. A stage poetry drama written by APRIL is showcased. APRIL, MIKE, HOMELESS 404, and TANG JIN
are singing a song while dancing like K-pop. APRIL wears a colorful hat made of ribbons, which reaches below her shoulders and pops up and down to the rhythm of rock and roll. In a minute, Chinese music "What a JASMINE Flower", is added, then African American and Spanish songs "You know how I get down", as well as robot songs and voices. In the end, APRIL gets on the stage and dances with long lanterns in her hands. Others stand and wave their arms and the audience cheers.

STAY ALIVE
Cathy Xinman

You May feel down

You may feel the challenge

See how we get down

You may feel up and down

See how we get down, down, down, no way

Let me show you how I get down

Get down to down payment

Get down to music and dance

See how we have a dream down, down, down,
no way

Vines and fig trees are on the hill.

We climb clap, clap, and clap

See how we get down I want to show you

They will bear fruit next year

Down the road

To eat and to live together

[fade out]

About Author

Cathy Xinman is a bilingual poet, screenwriter for film and stage, and winner of awards including the Golden Award at the San Francisco International New Concept Film Festival and the Remi Award. Her poetry received the first prize at the International Chinese Poetry Cup Competition. Her works include the poetry collection "Where You Love Yourself", "Flowers Kiss the Sun", a poetry writing guide, and the screenplay "Stay Alive" among others.

Contact

Email:xinmancathy@gmail.com

Email:cnawpress@gmail.com

Wechat: Xinman1225